THE SHEIKH AND THE SURROGATE MUM

BY
MEREDITH WEBBER

MILLS
BOON

First published in Great Britain 2012
by Mills & Boon, an imprint of Harlequin (UK) Limited.
Harlequin (UK) Limited, Eton House,
18-24 Paradise Road, Richmond, Surrey TW9 1SR

© Meredith Webber 2012

ISBN: 978 0 263 89196 6

Harlequin (UK) policy is to use papers that are natural, renewable and recyclable products and made from wood grown in sustainable forests. The logging and manufacturing process conform to the legal environmental regulations of the country of origin.

Printed and bound in Spain
by Blackprint CPI, Barcelona

'Beautiful,' she said.

'But not as beautiful as you,' he murmured, taking the beaker and draining the last drops. Then, with his lips still wet, he kissed her.

Liz was sure she didn't mean to kiss him back. She'd decided very firmly that kissing was off-limits where this man was concerned. Probably, in her condition, where *any* man was concerned! But she was definitely kissing him back—leaning into him, tasting the water on his lips, tasting him, wanting more while her head rambled on about not kissing men.

There was nothing simple about this kiss. If anything it was the most complex kiss Liz had ever experienced, for it seemed to be saying things as well as asking things, and she didn't understand any of it—except the need to keep on kissing Khalifa-whoever, His Highness of Al Tinine…

Meredith Webber says of herself, 'Once I read an article which suggested that Mills and Boon were looking for new Medical™ Romance authors. I had one of those "I can do that" moments, and gave it a try. What began as a challenge has become an obsession—though I do temper the "butt on seat" career of writing with dirty but healthy outdoor pursuits, fossicking through the Australian Outback in search of gold or opals. Having had some success in all of these endeavours, I now consider I've found the perfect lifestyle.'

CHAPTER ONE

'JUST because some bloke with more money than sense has bought the place, we don't need to go into a full-scale meltdown. He's bought the hospital, not our bodies and souls. We have to—'

Dr Elizabeth Jones was addressing her slightly panicked night shift staff outside the special care neonatal unit of Giles Hospital when a deep, slightly accented voice interrupted her.

'This word "bloke"? It means?'

She turned to face the source of the voice and her heart thudded to a halt, flopped around a bit and then went into a gallop rhythm she couldn't recall ever having felt before.

He wasn't drop-dead gorgeous, or even astoundingly good looking—he was just so, well, very *male*!

Arrogantly male!

His bearing, the slight tilt of his head, the imperious look in his near-black eyes, all shouted *leader of the pack*.

'Oh! Um—it's actually nothing. Aussie slang, you know—means a man...'

The words faltered out in dribs and drabs, her brain too busy cataloguing the stranger's attributes to construct sensible sentences.

Smooth olive skin, the slightest, neatest of clipped beards and moustache emphasising a straight nose and a strong jaw, not to mention framing lips like—well, she couldn't think how to describe the lips, although the words 'eminently kissable' had sneaked into her head.

He wore a dark suit, though the way he wore it—or maybe it was the suit itself—made her wonder if she'd ever really seen a man in a suit before.

'I see!' the lips she'd noticed before the suit mused. 'So the "bloke" who bought the hospital has more money than sense?'

It was the accent making her toes curl in her strappy sandals and sending feathery touches up and down her spine.

It *had* to be!

'It was a stupid thing to say,' Liz added, back in control. Almost. 'It's just that this particular hospital is hardly a money-making concern because part of the original trust that set it up ensures we treat a percentage of non-paying patients, although—'

She stopped before she insulted the man further—if this *was* the man with more money than sense—by assuming he'd change that rule. In fact, from the day the staff had learned the hospital was on the market they had all assumed it *would* be changed. After all, who in their right mind would invest in a business that ran at a loss?

Who would invest in a business that ran at a loss? Khalifa could see the words she didn't say flashing across her face.

An interesting face—arresting. Though maybe it was nothing more than the black-framed glasses that made it that way. What woman wore glasses with heavy black plastic frames these days? They did emphasise her clear creamy complexion but certainly didn't match her hair, ruthlessly restrained in a tidy knot behind her head, yet still revealing more than a hint of deep red in the darkness of it.

Intriguing, but he was here on business.

'I am the bloke you speak of, but I do not intend to make money from the hospital,' he assured her and the small group of staff who'd been her audience when he'd approached. 'I will continue to run it according to the original charter, but I hope to be able to bring some of the equipment up to date, and perhaps employ more staff.'

He paused. He'd intended outlining his plan to a meeting of the heads of the different departments, and had walked down to look again at the special care unit because it was his main interest. But now he was here, perhaps a less formal approach would be better.

Or did he want to spend more time studying the woman with the black glasses?

'My name is Sheikh Khalifa bin Saif al Zahn. Just Khalifa will suffice. I have bought the hospital in the hope that you, the staff, can help me and that I can, perhaps, offer those of you who wish to take part an interesting and hopefully enjoyable experience.'

The blank looks on the faces of the small group told him his explanation hadn't worked.

'I have built a new hospital in my homeland—an island state called Al Tinine—and it is operating well. My next wish is to set up a special care neonatal unit like this one. I am hoping to bring staff from my hospital to work here to gain an insight into how *you* work, and I would like to think some of the staff at this hospital would enjoy working for short periods in my country.'

He was certain this further explanation had been perfectly clear—perhaps the blank looks were caused by surprise.

Then the woman—he knew from photos she was Dr

Elizabeth Jones, the one he wanted most of all—although in the photos she hadn't had the ghastly glasses and hadn't looked quite so—attractive?—stepped forward, knocking a pile of papers from the top of a filing cabinet and muttering under her breath before holding out her hand. One of the other women began gathering the papers, tapping them into a neat pile.

'How do you do, Dr Khalifa?' Dr Jones said formally, adding her name. 'Forgive us for reacting like dumbstruck idiots, but it isn't often anyone takes notice of our small hospital, let alone wanders in and offers us a chance to visit other countries. As for new equipment, we should be dancing with glee and cheering wildly. We make do with what we have and our success rate here in the special care unit in particular is first class, but the money from the trust that set up the hospital has been running out for some years.'

Khalifa heard the words but his brain had stopped working.

The woman he wanted, now she'd stepped out from behind the filing cabinet on which she'd been leaning, was undoubtedly pregnant. Not a huge bump, but pregnant enough to notice.

The shadow of pain, the fiercer thrust of guilt that chased him through each day had registered the bump immediately.

Dr Elizabeth Jones was as pregnant as Zara had been the last time he'd seen her…

Realising he'd dropped the conversational ball, Dr Jones spoke again.

'It sounds a wonderful opportunity for our staff to travel to your country and I'm sure we'd be very happy to welcome staff from your hospital, to learn from them as well as show them how we do things.'

There was a slight frown creasing the creamy skin, as

if she wasn't absolutely certain of the truth of her words, but before he could decide, or even thank her for her kindness, a faint bell sounded and the group of women broke away immediately.

'Excuse me,' the doctor said. 'That was an end-of-shift meeting we were having. The new shift is on duty and I'm needed.'

She whisked away from the makeshift office—was one small desk and the filing cabinet in this alcove off the hall all they had?—and entered the glass-walled room where two lines of cribs held tiny babies. Two women— nurses, he assumed—in black and white patterned smocks leant over one of the cribs, straightening as Dr Jones joined them. Uncertain as to the isolation status of the ward, he remained outside, watching through the glass as she bent over the crib, touching the infant's cheek with one finger while reading the monitor beside it.

One of the nurses had wheeled a small trolley laden with drugs and equipment to the side of the crib but in the end Dr Jones straightened and shook her head, writing something on the chart at the end of the crib and stroking the baby's cheek, smiling down at the tiny being, before leaving the unit.

'You're still here!'

She spoke abruptly, obviously distracted by whatever it was that had summoned her to the baby's crib, then she proved his guess correct by adding, 'She has a little periodic apnoea but I don't want to put her back on CPAP.'

'Has she just come off it?' he asked, and the woman frowned at him.

'You understood that? I was really thinking out loud. Very rude, but I suppose if you've built one hospital and bought another, you probably do know a few things about medicine.'

'I know a few,' he said. 'Enough to get me through my medical degree and a follow-up in surgery.'

'I'm sorry,' she said, flashing a smile that almost hid a flush of embarrassment in her cheeks. 'It's just that health care seems to have become big business these days and the business owners don't necessarily know anything about medicine. But I'm holding you up. You'll want to see the rest of the place, and talk to staff in other departments, won't you?'

'Not right now,' he began, uncertain now that the woman's pregnancy had thrown his plans into disarray. 'You see, I'm particularly interested in this special care unit because I *had* hoped to persuade you to come to Al Tinine to set one up. I have heard and read so many good things about the work you do here, running a small unit that offers premature babies surprisingly successful outcomes on a limited budget.'

She studied him, her head tilted slightly to one side, and he wondered what she was seeing.

A foreigner in an expensive suit?

A bloke with more money than sense?

Guilty on both counts!

'So are you looking for something similar in size? Will there be limitations on the budget of the unit you wish to set up?'

Shocked by the assumption, he rushed into speech.

'Of course not—that wasn't what I meant at all. Naturally, we won't be looking at gold-plated cribs, but I would want you to have the very best equipment, and appropriate staffing levels, whatever you deemed necessary for the best possible outcomes for premature infants born in the southern part of my country.'

She smiled again—not much of a smile but enough

to light a spark in the wide blue eyes she hid behind the chunky glasses.

'Gold plate would probably be toxic anyway,' she said, then the smile slid away and the little crease of a frown returned. 'My next question would be, are you setting it up as a working, effective unit that will give preemie babies the very best chance of leading normal lives later on, or are you putting it in because you think hospitals should have one?'

The question shocked him even more than the previous assumption had, although would he have considered it if not for Zara's and the baby's deaths?

That thought angered him.

'Are you always this blunt?' he demanded, scowling at her now. 'I expect you to set up a properly organised special care neonatal unit with some facilities for infants who would, in a larger hospital, go into a neonatal intensive care unit. I understand you have such facilities in your unit here at Giles, which is one of the reasons I chose this hospital.'

No need to tell her that the other reason was because he'd heard and read such impressive reports of *her* work with neonates.

'Fair enough,' she said easily, apparently unperturbed by his scowl and growling reply. 'But when you said "you", did you mean "you" as in someone from the unit or me personally?'

Direct, this woman!

'I did mean you personally,' he told her, equally direct. 'It is you I wanted—or was you.'

'And having seen me, you've changed your mind?' The words were a challenge, one he could see repeated in the blue eyes for all she hid them behind those revolting glasses. 'Too tall? Too thin? Wrong sex, although the

Elizabeth part of my name must have been something of a clue?'

'You're pregnant.'

He spoke before he could consider the implication of his statement, and as her face flushed slightly and her eyes darkened with some emotion he couldn't read, he knew he'd made a mistake.

A big mistake!

'So?'

The word was as steely as the thrust of a well-honed sword, but as he struggled to parry the thrust she spoke again.

'Pregnancy is a condition, not an illness, as I'm sure you know. I have worked through the first thirty-two weeks and I intend to continue working until the baby is born, returning to work...'

The fire died out of her and she reached out to support herself on the filing cabinet behind which her 'condition' had originally been hidden. The air in the alcove had thickened somehow, and though he knew you couldn't inhale things like despair and sadness, that was how it tasted.

'Actually—' the word, her voice strong again, brought him back to the present '—a trip away right now might be just what the doctor ordered. I presume if you're setting up a neonatal unit you already have obstetricians and a labour ward so my having the baby there wouldn't be a problem. As far as this unit is concerned, we have visiting paediatricians who are rostered on call, plus there's a new young paediatrician just dying to take over my job, so it would all fit in.'

The steel was back in her voice and he wondered if it came from armour she'd built around herself for some reason. She'd shown no emotion at all when she'd talked about

her pregnancy, no softening of her voice, just a statement
of facts and enquiries about obstetric services.

Neither did she wear a wedding ring, although handling
tiny babies she probably wouldn't...

'Well?'

Liz knew she'd sounded far too abrupt, flinging the
word at him like that, but the idea of getting away from
the turmoil in her life had come like a lifeline thrown to a
drowning sailor. She was slowly learning to live with the
grief of Bill's death, but Oliver's continued existence in a
coma in this very hospital was a weight too heavy to carry,
especially as his parents had banned her from seeing him.

Oliver's state of limbo put her into limbo as well—her
and the baby—while the unanswerable questions just kept
mounting and mounting.

Would Oliver come out of the coma? Would his brain
be functioning if he did? And would he want the baby?

She sighed, then realised that the man had been speaking while she was lost in her misery.

'I'm sorry,' she said, and this time heard him asking
about passports and how soon she could leave the country.

'Right now, today!' she responded, then regretted
sounding so over-eager. 'To be fair, I'd need a week or
so to bring my replacement up to date. She's worked here
before, which is why she wanted to come back, so it won't
take much. And it's not as if I won't be coming back—
you're talking about my setting up the unit and getting it
running, not offering a permanent placement, aren't you?'

The man looked bemused, but finally he nodded,
though it seemed to her that his face had hardened and
the arrogance she'd sensed within him when he'd first
spoken had returned.

He didn't like her—not one bit.

'There is no one with whom you should discuss this first?' he asked.

Liz shrugged.

'Not really. Providing I leave the unit in good hands, the hospital hierarchy won't complain, and as you've probably already discussed your idea of staff swapping with them, they won't be surprised. And this first trip shouldn't take long, anyway. It will be a matter of organising space, equipment and staff. It's not as if you'll be taking in babies until those are all in place.'

Now he was frowning. It had to be the pregnancy. He obviously wasn't used to pregnant women working. Well, it was time he got used to it.

The silence stretched, so awkward she was wondering if she should break it, but what could she say to this stranger that wasn't just more chat? And though she certainly hadn't given that impression earlier, she really didn't do chat.

Relief flooded her as he spoke again.

'Very well. I will be in touch later today with a date and time for our departure. I have your details from the HR office. In the meantime, you might make a list of equipment you will require. My hospital is the same size as Giles, and I would anticipate the unit would be similar in size to this one.'

The words were so coldly formal Liz had to resist an impulse to drop a curtsey, but as the man wheeled away from her, she gave in to bad behaviour, poked out her tongue and put her thumbs to her ears, waggling her fingers at him.

'He'd have caught you if he'd turned around,' her friend Gillian said, before taking up what was really worrying her. 'And what on earth are you thinking? Agreeing to traipse off to a place you've never heard of, with a strange man, and pregnant, and with Oliver the way he is, not to mention leaving all of us in the lurch?'

Liz smiled. The sentiments may have been badly expressed but Gillian's concern for her was genuine. Could she explain?

'You know Oliver's family won't let me near him,' she began, 'and Carol is the perfect replacement, and she's available so no one's being left in the lurch. That said, what is it you're most worried about—the pregnancy, the strange man, or that I've never heard of this Al Tinine?'

'It's the decision,' Gilliam told her. 'Making it like that. It's totally out of character for you. You took months mulling over doing the surrogacy thing—could you do it, should you do it, would you get too attached to the baby? You asked yourself a thousand questions. And while I know you've been through hell these last few months, do you really think running away will help?'

Liz shook her head.

'Nothing will help,' she muttered, acknowledging the dark cloud that had enshrouded her since Bill's death, 'but if I'm going to be miserable, I might as well be miserable somewhere new. Besides, setting up a unit from scratch might be the distraction I need. I love this place, would bleed for it, but you know full well the staff could run it without much help from me, so it's hardly a challenge any more.'

'But the baby?'

Gillian's voice was hesitant, and Liz knew why. It was the question everyone had been wanting to ask since the accident that had killed her brother and put his partner in hospital, but the one subject they hadn't dared broach.

Liz shrugged her shoulders, the helplessness she felt about the situation flooding through her.

'I've no idea,' she admitted slowly. 'The accident wasn't

exactly part of the plan when I agreed to carry a baby for Bill and Oliver, and with Oliver the way he is and me not being able to even see him, who knows what happens next? Certainly not me! All I can do is keep going.'

She suspected she sounded hard and uncaring, but from the moment she'd agreed to carry a child for her brother and his partner, an agreement made, as Gillian had reminded her, after much soul-searching, she'd steeled herself not to get emotionally involved with a baby that would never be hers. She'd played it music Bill and Oliver loved, told it long stories about its parents, cautious always to remember it was their baby, not hers.

It would never be hers.

Now its future was as uncertain as her own, and she had no idea which way to turn. No wonder the challenge the man had offered had seemed like a lifeline—a tiny chink of light shining through the dark, enveloping cloud.

Then another thought struck her. Had the man said 'our' departure? Did he intend to hang around?

She felt a shiver travel down her spine, and her toes curled again...

Khalifa sat in the hospital's boardroom, listening to his lawyers speaking to their counterparts from the hospital, but his mind was on a woman with heavy-framed glasses, a pregnant woman who seemed totally uninvolved in her own pregnancy. Zara had been transformed by hers, overjoyed by the confirmation, then delighting in every little detail, so wrapped up in the changes happening in her body that any interest she might ever have had in her husband—not much, he had to admit—had disappeared.

To be fair to her, the arranged marriage had suited him as he'd been building the hospital at the time, busy with the thousand details that had always seemed to need his attention, far too busy to be dealing with wooing a woman. Later, Zara's involvement in her pregnancy had freed him from guilt that he spent so little time with her, though in retrospect...

He passed a hand across his face, wiping away any trace of emotion that might have slipped through his guard. Emotion weakened a man and the history of his tribe, stretching back thousands of years, proved it had survived because of the strength of its leaders. Now, in particular, with El Tinine taking its place among its oil-rich neighbours and moving into a modern world, he, the leader, had to be particularly strong.

'Of course we will do all we can to assist you in selecting the equipment you need for the new unit in your hospital,' the chief medical officer was saying. 'Dr Jones has updated our unit as and when funds became available. She knows what works best, particularly in a small unit where you are combining different levels of patient need. I'll get my secretary to put together a list of equipment we've bought recently and the suppliers' brochures. Dr Jones will be able to tell you why she made the choices she did.'

He hurried out of the room.

Dr Jones... The name echoed in Khalifa's head.

Something about the woman was bothering him, something that went beyond her apparent disregard for her pregnancy. Was it because she'd challenged him?

Not something Zara had ever done.

But Zara had been his wife, not his colleague, so it couldn't be that...

Was it because Dr Jones running from something—the father of her baby?—that she'd leapt at his offer to come to Al Tinine? There had been no consultation with anyone, no consideration of family or friends, just how soon could she get away.

Yes, she was running from something, it had to be that, but did it matter? And why was he thinking about her when he had so much else he hoped to achieve in this short visit?

It had to be her pregnancy and the memories it had stirred.

The guilt…

He, too, left the room, making his way back to the neonatal ward, telling himself he wanted to inspect it more closely, telling himself it had nothing to do with Dr Jones.

She was bent over the crib she'd been called to earlier and as she straightened he could read the concern on her face. She left the unit, sliding open the door and almost knocking him over in her haste to get to the little alcove.

'Sorry,' she said automatically, then stopped as she realised whom she'd bumped into. 'Oh, it's you! I *am* sorry— I'm a klutz, always knocking things over or running into people. My family said it was because I live in my head, and I suppose that's right at the moment. The baby in that crib was abandoned—found wrapped in newspaper in a park—and the police haven't been able to trace the mother. We call her Alexandra, after the park.'

Liz heard her rush of words and wondered what it was about this man that turned her into a blithering idiot, admitting to her clumsiness, thrusting ancient family history at a total stranger.

'The baby was found in a park?'

Despite the level of disbelief in the man's voice, her toes curled *again*. This was ridiculous. It had to stop. Probably it was hormonal…

'Last week,' she told him, 'and, really, there's nothing much wrong with her—she was a little hypothermic, occasional apnoea, but now…'

'Who will take her?'

Liz sighed.

'That's what's worrying me,' she admitted. 'She'll be taken into care. And while I know the people who care for babies and children are excellent, she won't get a permanent placement because she obviously has a mother somewhere. And right now when she desperately needs to bond with someone, she'll be going somewhere on a temporary basis.'

Why was she telling this stranger her worries? Liz wondered, frowning at the man as if he'd somehow drawn the words from her by...

Osmosis?

Magic?

She had no idea by what. Perhaps it was because he was here that she'd rattled on, because worrying about Alexandra was preferable to worrying about her own problems.

'You think the mother might return to claim her? Is that why the placement is temporary?'

Liz shook her head.

'I doubt she'll return to claim her. If she'd wanted her, why leave her in the first place? But if the authorities find the mother, they will do what they can to help her should she decide to keep the baby. It's a delicate situation but, whatever happens, until little Alexandra is officially given up for adoption, she'll be in limbo.'

Like me, Liz thought, and almost patted her burgeoning belly.

The man was frowning at her.

'You are concerned?' he asked.

'Of course I'm concerned,' Liz told him. 'This is a baby we're talking about. She's already had a rough start, so she deserves the very best.'

It didn't add up, Khalifa decided. This woman's attitude to a stranger's child, and her apparent disregard for her own pregnancy, although perhaps he was reading her wrongly. Perhaps this was her work face, and at home she talked and sang to her unborn child as much as Zara had to hers.

She *and* her partner talked and sang—

'Will the authorities also look for the baby's father?' he asked, and surprised a smile out of her.

'Harder to do, especially without the mother, although Alexandra's plight has been well publicised in local and interstate papers. The father may not have known the mother was pregnant. A man spends the night with a woman, and these days probably takes precautions, but there's no sign that flashes up in the morning, reminding him to check back in a few weeks to see if she's pregnant.'

There was no bitterness in the words and he doubted very much that her pregnancy had resulted from a chance encounter. Klutz she might be, but everything he'd read about her suggested she was very intelligent.

Though klutz?

'What's a klutz?'

Now she laughed, and something shifted in his chest.

Was it because the laughter changed her from a reasonably attractive woman to a beautiful one, lit from within by whatever delight the question had inspired?

Because the blue eyes he was drawn to behind the glasses were sparkling with humour?

He didn't think so. No, it was more the laughter itself—so free and wholesome—so good to hear. Did people laugh out loud less these days or was it just around him they were serious?

'It's a word we use for a clumsy person. I'm forever dropping things—not babies, of course—or knocking stuff over, or running into people. Hence the really, really horrible glasses. Rimless ones, thin gold frames, fancy plastic—I kill them all. Bumping into a door, or dropping them, or sitting on them, I've broken glasses in ways not yet invented. I tried contact lenses for a while but kept losing them—usually just one, but always the same one. So I had five right eyes and no left, which would have been okay for a five-eyed monster, of course. Anyway, now I go for the heaviest, strongest, thickest frames available. I'm a typical klutz!'

She hesitated, as if waiting for his comment on klutzdom, but he was still considering his reaction to her laughter and before he could murmur some polite assurance that she probably wasn't that bad, she was speaking again.

'Not that you need to worry about my work abilities, I'm always totally focussed when I'm on the job. In fact, that's probably my problem outside it—in my head I'm still in the unit, worrying about one or other of our small charges.'

Yes, he could understand that, but what he couldn't understand was how freely this woman chatted with a virtual stranger. Every instinct told him she wasn't a chatterer, yet here she was, rattling on about her clumsiness and monsters and an abandoned baby.

Was she using words to hide something?

Talking to prevent him asking questions?

He had no idea, but he'd come to see the unit, not concern himself with this particular employee.

Which was why he was surprised to hear himself asking if there was somewhere other than this alcove off the passageway where they could sit down and talk.

'Of course! We've got a canteen in the courtyard, really lovely, but I suppose you've seen it already. I'll just let someone know where I'll be.'

She stepped, carefully, around him and entered the unit, stopping to speak to one of the nurses then peering behind a screen and speaking to someone before joining him outside.

'How much space do you have at this new hospital of yours?' she asked, the little frown back between blue eyes that were now sombre.

He glanced back at the unit, measuring it in his mind.

'I've set aside an area, maybe twice the size of what you have here,' he told her, and was absurdly pleased when the frown disappeared.

'That's great,' she declared, clearly delighted. 'We can have decent, reclining armchairs for the visiting parents and a separate room where mothers can express milk or breastfeed instead of being stuck behind a tatty screen. Beginning breastfeeding is particularly hard for our mothers. The babies have been getting full tummies with absolutely no effort on their part because the milk comes down a tube. Then suddenly they're expected to work for it, and it's frustrating for both parties.'

She was leading him along a corridor, striding along and talking at the same time, her high-heeled strappy sandals making her nearly as tall as he was.

A pregnant woman in high-heeled strappy sandals?

A doctor at work in high-heeled strappy sandals?

Not that her legs didn't look fantastic in them…

What *was* he thinking!

It was the pregnancy thing that had thrown him. Too close to home—too many memories surfacing. If only he'd been more involved with Zara and the pregnancy, if only he'd been home more often, if only…

'Here,' his guide declared, walking into the leafy courtyard hung with glorious flowering orchids. 'This, as you can see, is a special place. Mr Giles, who left the bequest for the hospital, was a passionate orchid grower and these orchids are either survivors from his collection or have been bred from his plants.'

Khalifa looked around, then shook his head.

'I did notice the courtyard on one of my tours of the hospital, but didn't come into it. It's like an oasis of peace and beauty in a place that is very busy and often, I imagine, very sombre. I should have thought of something similar. I have been considering practicality too much.'

His companion smiled at him.

'Just don't take space out of my unit to arrange a courtyard,' she warned. 'Now, would you like tea or coffee, or perhaps a cold drink?'

'Let me get it, Dr Jones,' he said, reaching into his pocket for his wallet. 'You'll have...?'

'I'm limiting myself to one coffee a day so I make it a good one. Coffee, black and strong and two sugars, and it's Liz,' she replied, confusing him once again.

'Liz?' he repeated.

'Short for Elizabeth—Liz, not Dr Jones.'

He turned away to buy the coffees, his mind repeating the short name, while some primitive instinct sprang to life inside him, warning him of something...

But what?

'Two coffees, please. Strong, black and two sugars in both of them.'

He gave his order, and paid the money, but his mind was trying to grasp at the fleeting sensation that had tapped him on the shoulder.

Because of their nomadic lifestyle in an often hostile country, an instinct for danger was bred into him and all his tribal people, but this woman couldn't represent a danger, so that couldn't be it.

But as he took the coffees from the barista, the sensation came again.

It couldn't be because they drank their coffee the same way! Superstition might be alive and well in his homeland, but he'd never believed in any of the tales his people told of mischievous djinns interfering in people's lives, or of a conflagration of events foretelling disaster. Well, not entirely! And a lot of people probably drank their coffee strong and black with two sugars.

Besides, he only drank it this way when he was away from home. At home, the coffee was already sweet and he'd drink three tiny cups of the thick brew in place of one of these...

CHAPTER TWO

COULD ten days really have flown so quickly?

Of course, deciding on what clothes she should take had consumed a lot of Liz's spare time. Khalifa...could she really call him that? So far she'd avoided using his name directly, but if she was going to be working with him she'd have to use it some time.

Not that she didn't use it in her head, sounding it out, but only in rare moments of weakness, for even saying it started the toe curling—and she had to stretch them as hard as she could to prevent it happening.

Anyway, Khalifa had given her a pile of wonderful information brochures about his country, explaining that the capital, Al Jabaya, was in the north, and that his eldest brother, while he had been the leader, had, over twenty years, built a modern city there. The southern part of Al Tinine, however, was known as the Endless Desert, and the area, although well populated, had been neglected. It was in the south, in the oasis town of Najme, that Khalifa had built his hospital.

For clothes Liz had settled on loose trousers and long shift-like shirts for work, and long loose dresses for casual occasions or lolling around at home, wherever home turned out to be. Wanting to respect the local customs, she'd made sure all the garments were modest, with sleeves and high necklines.

Now here she was, in a long, shapeless black dress—black so it wouldn't show the things she was sure to spill on herself on a flight—waiting outside her apartment block just as the sun was coming up. Gillian, who would house—and cat-sit, waited beside her.

'Your coach approaches, Cinderella,' Gillian said, as a sleek black limousine turned into the street.

'Wrong fairy-tale, Gill,' Liz retorted. 'Mine's the one with Scheherazade telling the Sultan story after story so she didn't get her head chopped off next morning.'

Had she sounded panicked that Gill looked at her with alarm?

'You're not worrying *now* about this trip, are you? Haven't you left it a bit late? What's happened? You've been so, well, not excited but alive again.'

The vehicle pulled up in front of them before Liz could explain that sheer adrenalin had carried her this far, but now she was about to depart, she wasn't having second thoughts but third and fourth and fifth right down to a thousandth.

Better not to worry Gill with that!

'I'm fine,' she said, then felt her toes curl and, yes, he was there, stepping smoothly out of the rear of the monstrous car just as she tripped on the gutter and all but flung herself into his arms.

He was quick, she had to give him that—catching her elbow first then looping an arm around her waist to steady her.

She'd have been better off falling, she decided as her body went into some kind of riotous reaction that was very hard to put down to relief that she *hadn't* fallen!

'You must look where you are going,' he said, but although the words came out as an order, his voice was gruff with what sounded like concern.

For her?

How could she know?

And did it really matter?

The driver, meanwhile, had picked up her small case and deposited it in the cavernous trunk so there was nothing else for Liz to do but give Gill a quick kiss goodbye and step into the vehicle.

In the back.

With Khalifa.

'Wow, look at the space in here. I've never been in a limo!' she said, while her head reminded her that it had been years since she'd talked like a very young teenager. Perhaps she was better saying nothing.

'Would you like a drink? A cold soda of some kind?'

Khalifa had opened a small cabinet, revealing an array of beverages. The sight of them, and the bottles of wine and champagne—this at six-thirty in the morning—delighted Liz so much she relaxed and even found a laugh.

'You're talking to a klutz, remember. I can just imagine the damage a fizzy orange drink could do to this upholstery. Besides, I've just had my coffee fix so I should manage an hour's drive to the airport without needing further refreshment.'

It was the laugh that surprised him every time, Khalifa realised. He hadn't heard it often in the last ten days but every time it caught his attention and he had to stop himself from staring at his new employee, her face transformed to a radiant kind of beauty by her delight in something. Usually something absurd.

'So tell me about Najme,' she said, a smile still lingering on her lips and what sounded like genuine interest in her voice.

He seized the opportunity with both hands. Talking about Najme, his favourite place on earth, was easy.

And it would prevent him thinking about his companion and the way she affected him—especially the way she'd affected him when he'd caught her in his arms…

'Najme means star. It has always been considered the star of the south because of the beauty of the oasis on which it is built. Date palms flourish there, and grass and ferns, while reeds thrive by the water's edge. When oil was discovered, because Al Jabaya was a port from ancient times, used for trading vessels and the pearling fleet, it seemed right that the capital should be built there. So my brother and his advisors laid out plans and the city grew, but it virtually consumed all his time, and the south was not exactly neglected but left behind. Now it is up to me to bring this area into the twenty-first century, but I must do it with caution and sensitivity.'

He looked out the window as the sleek vehicle glided along a motorway, seeing houses, streets, shops and factories flash by. It was the sensitivity that worried him, bringing change without changing the values and heritage of his people.

It was because of the sensitivity he'd married Zara, a young woman of the south, hoping her presence by his side would make his changes more acceptable.

And then he'd let her down…

'Is the hospital your first project there?' his colleague asked. Pleased to be diverted, he explained how his brother had seen to the building of better housing, and schools right across the country, and had provided free medical care at clinics for the people in the south, but he had deemed the hospital in Al Jabaya to be sufficient for the country, even providing medical helicopters to fly people there.

'But the people of Najme, all the people of the south, have always been wary of the northerners. The southern regions were home to tribes of nomads who guarded trade routes and traded with the travellers, providing fresh food and water, while Al Jabaya has always been settled. The Al Jabayans were sailors, pearl divers and also traders, but their trade has been by sea, so they have always been in contact with people of other lands. They are more... worldly, I suppose you would say.'

'And you?'

The question was gentle, as if she sensed the emotion he felt when talking of his people.

'My mother was from the south. My brother's mother was from the north, so when she grew old, my father took a second wife—actually, I think she was the third but that's not talked of often. Anyway, for political reasons he took a wife from a southern tribe, so my ties are to the south. My wife, too, was a southerner...'

He stopped, aware he'd spoken to no one about Zara since her death, and none of his friends had used her name—aware, no doubt, that it was a subject he wouldn't discuss.

'Your wife,' Liz Jones prompted, even gentler now.

'She died in childbirth. The baby was premature, and she, too, died.'

Liz heard the agony in his voice, and nothing on this earth could have prevented her resting her hand on his.

'So of course you want the unit. It will be the very best we can achieve.' She squeezed his fingers, just a comforting pressure. 'I know it won't bring back your wife or child, but I promise you it will be a fitting memorial to them and be something you'll be proud of.'

Then, feeling utterly stupid, she removed her hand and tucked it in her lap lest it be tempted to touch him again.

This time the silence between them went beyond awkward and, aware she'd overstepped a boundary of some kind, Liz had no idea how to ease the tension. She leaned forward, intending to take a drink from the cabinet—but as she'd already pointed out, spilling fizzy orange soda all over the seat and undoubtedly splashing her new boss probably wasn't the answer.

Instead, she pulled one of the information leaflets he'd given her from her capacious handbag and settled back into the corner to read it. If he wanted the silence broken, let him break it.

He didn't, and, determined not to start blithering again, she refused to comment when the car sailed past the wide road that led to the international air terminal. Sailed past the road to the domestic one as well, then turned into another road that led to high wire fences and a gate guarded by a man in a security uniform.

To Liz's surprise, the man at the gate saluted as the gates swung open, and the limo took them out across wide tarmac to stop beside a very large plane, its sleek lines emphasised by the streaks and swirls of black and gold paint on its side. It took her a moment to recognise the decoration as Arabic script and she could be silent no longer.

'What does it say?' she asked, totally enthralled by the flowing lines, the curves and squiggles.

'Najme,' her host replied, and before she could ask more, he was out of the limo and speaking to some kind of official who waited at the bottom of the steps.

The driver opened the door on Liz's side and she slid out, not as elegantly as her companion had but, thankfully, without falling flat on her face.

'This gentleman will stamp your passport and one of my pilots will check your luggage,' Khalifa told her, all business now. 'It is a precaution he has to take, I'm sure you understand.'

Totally out of her depth, Liz just nodded, grateful really that she had no decisions to make. She handed over her passport, then hovered near the bottom of the steps until a young man came down and invited her inside.

'Khalifa will bring your passport and the pilot will put your luggage on board,' he told her. 'I am Saif, Khalifa's assistant. On flights I act as steward. He prefers not to have strangers around.'

Liz smiled to herself, certain the young man had no idea just how much he'd told her about his master. But there was no time to dwell on these little details for she'd reached the top of the steps, and entered what seemed like another world.

There was nothing flashy about the interior of the plane, just opulent comfort, with wide, well-padded armchairs in off-white leather, colourful cushions stacked on them, and more, larger, flat cushions on the floor near the walls of the aircraft. A faint perfume hung in the air, something she couldn't place—too delicate to be musk, more roses with a hint of citrus.

'Sit here,' Saif said, then he waited until she sank obediently into one of the armchairs before showing her where the seat belt was and how a small table swung out from beside the chair and a monitor screen opened up on it.

'You will find a list of the movies and other programmes in the book in the pocket on the other side of the chair, and you can use your laptop once we're in the air. Press this button if there's anything you require and I will do my best to help you.'

Saif turned away, and Liz realised Khalifa had entered the plane. He came towards her, enquired politely about her comfort, handed back her passport then took the chair on the other side of the plane.

'All this space to carry two people?' she asked, unable to stop herself revealing her wonder in the experience.

'It can be transformed into many configurations,' Khalifa replied. 'The flight time is fifteen hours, and I thought you might be more comfortable in a bed, so the back of the cabin is set up for your convenience.'

'With a bed?'

It went beyond Scheherazade's fantastic stories, and now Liz forgot about hiding her wonder.

'I've read about executive jets, but never thought I'd experience anything like this. May I have a look?'

Was it the excitement in her voice that stirred the man? She had no idea, but at least he'd smiled, and as she felt a slight hitch in her breathing, she told herself it was better that he remained remote and unreachable—far better that he didn't smile.

'Wait until we're in the air. The aircraft door is closed and I assume the pilot is preparing for take-off. Because we have to compete with both the international and the domestic flights for take-off slots, we can't delay. But while we're on the ground, Saif could get you a drink. Perhaps champagne to celebrate your first flight in an executive jet?'

'I can celebrate with orange juice,' Liz said, and although Khalifa was sure he saw her right hand move towards her stomach, she drew back before she touched it. The mystery of her pregnancy—or her attitude to it—deepened. He'd seen a lot of Liz Jones in the last ten days, and not by even the slightest sign had she acknowledged the baby she carried.

Neither had she ever mentioned the baby's father, and

although he had a totally irrational desire to know about this unknown man, he couldn't bring himself to ask.

Oh, he'd thought of a dozen ways he could bring it up. *Does the baby's father not mind your leaving now? If you're still in my country, would the baby's father like to fly to Al Tinine for the birth?*

But every time he thought of a question, he told himself it was none of his business and quashed the desire to ask.

And it *was* none of his business, apart from the fact that the woman was coming to work for him and he'd have liked to know what made her tick. Having seen her in action in the Giles neonatal unit, he knew she was deeply involved with all her little charges, and genuinely caring, which made her apparent detachment from her own pregnancy all the more puzzling.

An enigma, that's what she was.

Saif had returned with freshly squeezed orange juice for them both and she smiled as she thanked him—smiled the kind of smile he'd seen her use around the unit, the smile she gave the other staff, the parents and the babies.

And just as irrationally as his desire to know about her baby's father came the thought that he'd like her to smile like that at him...

She'd pulled some papers out of the bag she'd carried on board, and as she sipped her juice she was studying them.

In order to avoid conversation?

The thought aggravated him. Most women he'd had aboard his plane had been only too keen to talk to him.

But, then, most women he'd had aboard his plane had been diversions—pleasant playmates—not work colleagues, and pregnant work colleagues at that.

And, come to think of it, the days of pleasant playmates were long gone, too.

Though surely the woman had *some* conversation.

'The baby in the unit, Alexandra,' he began, deciding he'd start one himself. 'Was anything sorted out for her?'

As the delightful smile flashed across Liz Jones's face he regretted his impulse, because having had it directed at him once, he immediately wanted to see her smile again, to keep her smiling.

'Alexandra's grandmother turned up. It was like a miracle. The woman was from Melbourne and her daughter had taken off around Australia, backpacking with a group of friends. Her mother, Rose her name is, suspected there was something wrong with her daughter, who'd been moody and unhappy even while she was planning her trip. It was only when Rose saw something on the television about Alexandra that she began to put the pieces of the puzzle together.'

Khalifa tried to picture the scenario. In his family, many of the women still lived together, three generations, sometime more, and other women in the family visited every day for breakfast or coffee. His grandmother would have picked up a pregnancy in an instant.

'Was this daughter living with her mother?' he asked, intrigued now. 'Or seeing her regularly? Would the mother not have noticed her pregnancy?'

He won another smile, only a small one but still it felt like a victory.

'Her daughter had always been big, and had put on more weight, but she hadn't been obviously pregnant before she'd left on the trip. She'd kept in contact with her mother, so Rose knew she'd been with her friends in Brisbane at the time Alexandra was found, but left almost immediately afterwards. By the time Rose saw the appeal for information, the daughter was in Central Australia somewhere, and, from photos sent on the mobile phone, considerably thinner.'

'And this Rose contacted you?'

'She phoned the hospital while the programme was still running on her television. She'd tried to phone her daughter but couldn't get through, but Rose turned out to be a determined woman and no grandchild of hers was going to be brought up in care. She offered to have a DNA test the next day and get the lab to send the results straight to the hospital, but even before she knew for certain, she was on a plane to Brisbane.'

'And she *is* the grandmother?'

Was he really so interested in one tiny baby, Liz wondered, or was he talking to divert her as the plane was rising smoothly into the sky? She had no idea, but Rose and Alexandra's story was a good one, so she continued to explain.

'She not only is, but she's a force to be reckoned with. She slashed her way through all the red tape, parried any objections and took her grandchild back to Melbourne yesterday. She says it's up to her daughter to decide what they tell Alexandra—she's keeping her name, too but Rose is more than happy to bring the infant up as her own.'

'So, a happy ending all round,' Khalifa said with a broad smile, and Liz forgot about toes curling because this smile was enough to make her entire body spark and fizz in a most unseemly manner.

She'd heard about physical attraction but had obviously never experienced it, because this was something entirely new, and entirely ridiculous because she was going to be working with this man and couldn't go around all sparky and fizzy every time he smiled.

Although perhaps he wouldn't smile too often!

'It *was* a happy ending,' she said, 'and a great relief as far as I am concerned as I'd have hated to go away leaving Alexandra in limbo.' She hesitated, then the words she knew she shouldn't say came out anyway. 'It's not a very comfortable place, limbo!'

She turned her attention back to the papers in on lap, although she knew their contents by heart. She hadn't needed to check out neonatal units on the internet, as she'd always kept up with latest developments, but she didn't want to get anything wrong or miss out on something that might work in Al Tinine.

Al Tinine... If Najme meant star, did Tinine also have a meaning? She pulled out the little table Saif had shown her and set down her file on the new unit, digging into her bag for the brochures on the country, certain there'd be an explanation somewhere.

She could ask.

But asking meant starting another conversation and having a conversation meant looking at him, and while she was looking at him he might smile and...

Klutz!

As far as she could remember, she'd never been a mental klutz, confining her clumsiness to the physical, but now her mind was running wild and bumping into things and losing the plot completely.

Could she put it down to a slight release from the grief and tension of the last few months?

She had no idea but hopefully it would sort itself out before too long and return to the focussed, professional brain she would need to do her job.

And to work out what was going to happen to the poor baby!

Surreptitiously, hiding her hand under the papers still resting on what was left of her lap, she gave it a pat, mentally reassuring it that things would sort themselves out, though what things, and quite how, she had no idea. Oliver was, after all, the father of the baby, and should he want it, and be fit enough to care for it, then all would be well, but there were too many uncertainties to even consider the poor thing's future at the moment so, to distract herself from the depression she was teetering towards, she forgot about not talking to Khalifa.

'The name, Tinine, does it, too, mean something?'

Of course he *had* to smile!

And now she was reasonably close to him, she could see a twinkle in the depths of his dark eyes.

A very beguiling twinkle.

Fizz, spark, spark, fizz—surely pregnant women shouldn't feel this level of physical attraction!

'You will have to wait and see,' he replied, and the promise in his voice made her physical reactions worse— far worse—though all the man was discussing was the name of his country, not some riotous sexual encounter in the back cabin of the plane.

Was it a double bed?

Queen size?

King?

Her wayward mind was throwing up the questions and it took all her determination and discipline to pull it back into line.

Forget about the destination, concentrate on the unit. She pulled out the figures, playing with what she already knew. Najme had a population of approximately fifty thousand people and a high birth rate of twenty per thousand. Khalifa had already explained that about a third of the population were expats, doctors, teachers, scientists and labourers, all brought in from other places to help in the modernisation of the country.

Fiddling with the figures, knowing full well that they told her only three basic beds would be required, she began to wonder just why her new boss was planning a larger facility.

'Are you expecting the population to grow fairly swiftly, or more people to move into the city? Or is there some other reason you want the larger unit?'

The question had come out before she realised Khalifa was speaking to Saif.

'I'm sorry, I shouldn't have interrupted. I was thinking out loud.'

No smile this time, which was just as well—and the little twinge of disappointment was stupidity.

'I'm discussing our menu for the flight and you're thinking work,' Khalifa said, enough amusement in his voice to start the fizzing. 'Do you never relax?'

'It's Tuesday, that's a workday for me. And, yes, I can relax, but I did want to check over these figures again.'

He almost smiled.

'The surrounding area supports probably as many people again, although the majority of them are living as they've always lived. Traditions dating back thousands of years are hard to change, and I am afraid if I rush things, we will lose too much.'

'Lose too much?' she queried.

'Traditional skills and values,' he said. 'I don't mean camel milking, or even spinning thread from the wool of goats, but what we call our intangible cultural heritage. The patterns the women wove into the rugs told the history of our tribe, told it in pictures they understood, and using these rugs, which they spread on the floor in summer and hung on the inside walls of their tents in winter, they taught the children. Now the children learn in school, learn skills and information they will need to equip them for the modern world. But how do we keep our tribal history alive?'

'You've spoken before about keeping tradition alive,' Liz remembered, 'and while I can't help you with any ideas about the cultural side, I do wonder, if these people live as they've always lived, will they use a hospital to have their babies, and would they be able to adapt to the situation if the baby needs special care?'

Her companion sighed deeply.

'I'm not really expecting them to use an obstetrician and have their babies in a hospital. Not immediately anyway, but once a baby is born, that life is precious and if it needs help, I am certain they will seek it.'

He paused and she wondered just how much pain this discussion might be causing him—how much it might remind him of his wife.

'We have always had midwives, for want of a better word: women within the tribe who were taught by their elders to help other women through their pregnancy and childbirth. Now young local women are training not only as modern midwives but as obstetricians, and although they can't be everywhere, they can work with the older women, explaining new ideas and methods. Maybe through them we can introduce the idea of special care for fragile infants so, should the situation arise, the women will more readily accept the unit.'

'Or perhaps, with a translator—even with you if you had the time—I could visit some of these outlying areas, take a crib, show them what we can do, and how we can help the babies, explain that the family can be involved as well.'

To Liz's surprise, the man laughed, a real, wholehearted laugh that changed his face completely.

'Not families, I implore you,' he said at last, still smiling. 'You will get aunts, cousins, sisters, grandmothers— forty or fifty people all wanting to sit with the baby.'

'That many?' Liz teased, smiling back at him, and something in the air stilled, tension joining them together in an invisible bond, eyes holding eyes, a moment out of time, broken only when Saif said, in a long-suffering voice, 'If we could please get back to the menu!'

The menu proved delicious. Slices of melon and fresh, sweet strawberries with a slightly tart mint syrup poured over them. Delicate slivers of duck breast followed, the slices arranged on overlapping circles of potato, crispy on top and soft underneath, while fresh white asparagus with a simple butter sauce completed the main meal.

Offered a range of sweets, Liz declined, settling instead for a platter of fruit and hard cheese, finding, to her delight, that the dates accompanying it were so delicious she had to comment on them.

'They are from Najme,' Khalifa explained. 'We have the best dates in the world.'

Liz, replete and happy, forgot about the moment of tension earlier and had to tease again.

'You'd know that, of course, from the World Date Olympics, would you? Do they judge on colour and size as well as taste?'

Khalifa studied her for a moment. Where was the stressed, anxious, and obviously sad woman he'd first met at the hospital? Was this light-hearted, teasing Liz Jones the real Liz Jones?

He had no idea, although the thought that she might have relaxed because she'd escaped from the father of her child did sneak into his mind.

'We just know ours are the best,' he said firmly, 'and while we don't have a date Olympics you'll be arriving just in time for the judging of the falcons—a kind of falcon Olympics.'

Interest sparked in her eyes and she studied him in turn—checking to see if he was joking?

'Falcons?' she repeated.

'Our hunting birds,' he explained. 'It's one custom we are determined not to let die. The birds are part of our heritage and at Najme you will see them at their best, for everyone wants to have the best bird.'

'Falcons,' she whispered, smiling, not at him, he thought, but to herself. 'Now I really know I'm heading for another world. Thank you,' she said, 'not just for giving me this opportunity but for so much else.'

She pushed aside the little table and undid her seat belt.

'And now,' she said, 'if it's all right with you, I might check out that bedroom.'

Saif must have been watching from behind the front curtain, for he appeared immediately, taking Liz's arm and leading her into the cabin.

And, no, he, Khalifa bin Saif Al Zahn, was not jealous of Saif walking so close to her.

Why should he be?

The woman was nothing more than another employee, if a somewhat intriguing one.

But as he remembered a moment earlier when they'd both smiled and something in the atmosphere around them had shifted, he knew that wasn't entirely true.

CHAPTER THREE

SHE was sleeping soundly when he knocked quietly and entered the cabin some hours later. Her lustrous hair was loose, spread across the pillow, a rich, red-brown—more red, he felt, but a deep, almost magenta red.

Beautiful against the white of the pillow and the rich cream of her skin, her hair was shiny, silky—his fingers tingled with a desire to feel the texture.

He moved into the cabin, slightly embarrassed at having to invade her privacy, and more than a little embarrassed by his thoughts. But the pilot had warned they were approaching turbulence, and Khalifa didn't want her thrown out of the bed. It was fitted with what in a chair would be called seat belts, simple bands that stretched across the bed to restrain a sleeping passenger.

Could he strap her in without disturbing her?

Was it even right to be doing this?

He wondered if he should wake her and let her do it herself, but she seemed so deeply asleep, and the little lines of worry he'd sometimes noticed on her face were smoothed away, the creamy skin mesmerising against the dark, rich swathe of hair.

No, he certainly shouldn't be looking at her as he strapped her in! He found the far side restraint and drew it across the bed and over her body, curled on its side, the bulge of her pregnancy resting on the mattress, one leg drawn up to balance her weight.

He picked up the other end of the strap, and clicked the belt shut, then tightened it, just slightly, so it would hold her firmly if the plane dropped suddenly, but not put pressure on her belly.

Even under the sheet he could make out the shape of her, but his eyes were drawn to her face, vulnerable somehow without the dark-framed glasses, an attractive face, full of strength and determination, though he'd seen it soften when she'd spoken of the baby, Alexandra.

But not when she mentioned her own pregnancy.

He had to leave.

Heaven forbid she woke and found him staring at her.

Yet his feet seemed rooted to the floor, his eyes feasting on the woman, not lasciviously at all, just puzzled that she remained such a mystery to him.

Puzzled that he *was* puzzled, for of course she was a mystery to him—he barely knew her.

And probably never would.

Looking at her isn't going to help you, he told himself, and after checking the cabin was free of loose objects that could fly about in turbulence, he did leave the room, but reluctantly.

Returning to his seat, he began to wonder if he'd made a big mistake, taking this woman to his homeland.

But why?

Having been educated in the West, he accepted equality in all things between men and women. A different equality existed in his own land, but never, in the history of the tribe, had women been seen as inferior for they were the carriers of history, the heart of the family, the heart of the tribe, so it wasn't the fact that she was a woman…

Except that it was!

Not only was she a woman but she was a woman who, for some totally perverse reason, he found attractive.

Extremely attractive.

Physically attractive.

Could he put it down to prolonged celibacy after Zara's death? Prolonged celibacy brought on by guilt that he'd not been there for her—not been closer to her—close enough to realise his own wife had been in trouble with her pregnancy...

Memories of the time made him wince and put the woman on the bed right out of his mind. Having failed one pregnant woman, he had no intention of getting involved with another one. She was an employee like any other, and he could treat her as such. Right now he had a mountain of work to get through, business matters that he'd set aside while he was in Australia.

Quickly absorbed in the details of a new university for Najme, in the number of departments the fledgling institution would have and the balance of staffing, he was surprised to find five hours had passed. The turbulence was also behind them, although when he shifted in his seat, wondering what movement had distracted him, a different turbulence made its presence felt.

Internal turbulence.

Liz Jones was standing in the doorway of the cabin, dark, red-brown hair tousled around her face, her eyes unfocussed as she cleaned her glasses with a tissue.

'I'm sorry to disturb you,' she said, stepping cautiously forward, 'but I need my bag to have a wash and fix my hair.'

'You might be more comfortable if you leave it down for the rest of the flight,' Khalifa heard himself say, although he knew he wasn't thinking of her comfort but of the glory of that shining tumble of hair.

I might be more comfortable if I'd never stepped onto this plane, never met this man, let alone agreed to travel to his country, Liz thought, but, contrarily enough, excitement was stirring in her. Refreshed by the sleep, all the doubts and questions left behind, she was now looking forward to whatever adventure this strange new country would offer her.

Once she was off the plane, that was.

Once she was away from the man who was having such a strange effect on her body.

Distracted by *that* thought, she grabbed only one of the handles of her bag, so as she lifted it the contents tumbled out, spilling files, and toiletries, her wallet and passport, her hairbrush and—

Her boss was out of his seat immediately, helping retrieve the scattered items, seeking out coins that had rolled away.

'Don't worry about the change, it will be useless in Al Tinine anyway,' Liz told him, totally mortified by the mess and sorry she'd ever mentioned being a klutz, as this was surely proving her point to him.

She scooped things into the bag, ramming them in any old how, until he held out the photo, grabbed at the last minute from her bedside table, still in its silver frame. Bill and Oliver, arms around each other, laughing as she'd snapped them...

Her companion was looking at it, perhaps a little puzzled, and she could hardly snatch it from his hand no matter how much she'd have liked to.

In the end, he passed it to her and she ran her finger, as she'd done a thousand times before, over Bill's image. The three of them had been surfing at Coolangatta when the photo had been taken.

'He was my brother, Bill,' she found herself saying.

'More than a brother, really. Our parents died in the World Trade Center in 2001. They were on holiday in New York, a cousin worked in the building and they'd gone in to have a look. I was in my second year at university, and Bill and his partner Oliver became my lifeline—the only family I had left. Then three months ago Bill was in a fatal motor vehicle accident. That's what the policeman said when he told me, not a car crash—nothing that simple—but a fatal motor vehicle accident, as if Bill was already a statistic of some kind.'

She slumped into the chair, as memories of that moment—memories she'd never shared with anyone—came flooding back.

I will not cry, she promised the image of her beloved brother. I might have blurted all that out to a stranger but I *will not cry*!

She breathed deeply, recovering her equilibrium, willing the tears she knew had welled in her eyes to not betray her by brimming over and sliding down her cheeks. And then she felt better—not only for now, as in not so teary, but better all through, somehow.

'I'm sorry,' she said to her companion, aware he was watching her intently, although those dark eyes revealed nothing in the way of emotion. 'I haven't talked about it much. Now I'd better tidy up.'

She made sure she had both handles of her bag in her hand and stood up, escaping as rapidly as she could without actually running to the cabin at the rear of the plane. She had a wash and tidied her hair, pulling it back into a low knot on the nape of her neck so she could relax back against the seat.

What she'd have liked to do next was hide away in this cabin, but she'd never been a coward.

She strode back in and took her seat, tucking her bag

with its memories in a compartment to one side. Khalifa
nodded acknowledgement of her return, and turned back
to the papers on the table in front of him almost immediately, making it plain he didn't expect to be engaged in
conversation.

Which was a good thing, as most of her conversations
with him led down paths she didn't want to follow. She
spread out her own papers, the ones about the size of units
for different population figures. In all, they needed three
spaces. One in the labour ward but surely they'd have that
already—a care corner for the newborn.

Or would they?

Intent now on the project, she forgot about not engag-
ing him in conversation.

'Do you already have a newborn care corner in the labour rooms and operating theatres?'

He looked across at her, frowning slightly.

'I beg your pardon?'

She *knew* she shouldn't have spoken!

'I'm sorry, I'm thinking through what you'll need, beginning with the infant's birth. I'm sure you do have an
area where immediate care can be provided, and possibly a neonatal stabilisation unit close by where low birth
weight or fragile newborns can be stabilised. These two
centres are not really part of the unit because they have to
be in or close by the labour rooms, but they come under
the director of the neonatal unit at most hospitals, including Giles, so I wondered.'

Was she making sense?

She was talking work, at which she was more than com-
petent, yet this man seemed to undermine her confidence
in herself to the extent that she always sounded as if she
was babbling at him.

Was it his stillness that threw her into turmoil? The air of other-worldliness he wore like an invisible cloak?

'I'm sorry,' he said, smiling—how she wished he wouldn't, and apparently the sleep hadn't help the fizzing or the sparking or her toes. 'I was involved in plans for a university and thinking of disciplines and staffing. I don't want to duplicate everything we already have at Al Jabaya, although some degree courses, like science, teaching and nursing, should be available at both. But to answer your question, we do have a newborn care corner in all the labour rooms, and we use that corner for stabilisation as well. Without a special care neonatal unit, up till now babies needing special care are airlifted to the hospital in the capital, which is very traumatic for the mother and the rest of the family.'

He really cares about things like that, Liz realised, hearing the depth of emotion in his voice. It made her want to like the man—but liking him, given the unexpected physical attraction, was probably not a good idea.

'So we'll need a stabilisation room and experienced staff for it. The equipment is much the same as we'll have in the unit, a crib with a radiant warmer, oxygen, a hand-operated neonate resuscitator, suction pump, examination light, laryngoscope set, and all the usual renewable equipment. I think two cribs in there would be enough, and with the provision for hand washing and infection control—bins, etc.—you'd need close to a hundred square feet. Is that doable?'

'It will be,' he said, and she heard it as a promise and wondered just how it must feel to be able to decide you wanted something then go right ahead and get it, or get it done. He'd wanted a neonatal paediatrician and here she was on a flight to a place she'd never heard of two weeks ago.

He'd lost her, Khalifa realised. She'd returned from the cabin and slid into her seat, and though he'd longed to talk to her—to ask more about the tragedies in her life, and things that weren't tragedies—he knew he had to respect her silence. In all truth, he knew silence was best, because he couldn't understand his desire to know more and that bothered him more than anything.

Then she'd asked a question and when he could have kept her talking because even if the talk was work re-lated, hearing her voice gave him pleasure, but, no, he'd cut her off with one short sentence and now the opportunity was gone.

Telling himself this was for the best didn't work, and the words and numbers on the pages in front of him danced around so he could make no sense of them at all. Fortunately, Saif came in, offering light snacks, telling their guest about mint tea which, he felt, would refresh her.

'Or perhaps you would like to try mint lemonade,' he said.

'Mint tea sounds lovely,' Liz told him, smiling so nat-urally at him that once again Khalifa felt a twist of what he refused to consider was jealousy.

Saif returned with the tea and crescent-shaped almond biscuits dusted with icing sugar, a delicacy he knew was Khalifa's weakness. Liz relaxed back in her seat as she sipped the tea, and nibbled on a biscuit. It meant that, with-out being too obvious about it, he could watch her—see her in profile—a high forehead and long straight nose, full lips, a darkish pink against her creamy skin, slightly open at rest, and a chin that suggested she'd hold her own in any argument.

The shapeless garment she wore—so like the all-con-cealing gowns he knew from home—was made of fine enough material for it to lie softly on her body, showing him the shape of heavy breasts and the bulge of her pregnancy, her body, hidden though it was, so obviously lush and ripe.

It *had* to be the celibacy—not actually deliberate, although early on his guilt over not spending enough time with Zara before her death had certainly meant he'd not looked at another woman. After her death he'd thrown himself into work, continuing to learn exactly what it meant to be leader of his country, and an affair had been the last thing on his mind.

As it was now, he told himself firmly, but just as he forced himself to make sense of the words on the papers on front of him, the distraction in the plane with him spoke again.

'Leaving the stabilisation unit for the moment, the rule of thumb for a neonatal unit is three beds for every thousand deliveries, so realistically we'd only need three beds. If we add one or perhaps two critical-care beds to that, and another two for babies that might be brought in from elsewhere, we're up to six or seven, with two in the stabilisation unit. I know I should wait and see the space, but I'm thinking if it's close enough to the labour rooms for us to handle the stabilisation, perhaps in a divided-off corner of the neonate unit, it would ease any staff pressures and make the whole unit more financially viable.'

Was she as involved in this as she sounded, or was she attempting to sound detached because the brief glimpse of her life she'd revealed earlier had embarrassed her?

He guessed it would have. Even on such brief acquaintance he was reasonably certain she was not a woman who would confide in any but the closest of friends. So telling him about her brother had been a sign she was unsettled.

Because she was on her way to an unknown destination?

Or because of him?

He *had* to concentrate on work.

'Don't worry about financial considerations—stick to what you feel will work best.'

She flashed a smile in his direction.

'That's a dangerous statement to make, but I won't spend your money foolishly. We don't want staff hanging around doing nothing, because they'd become bored, and bored staff can let something slip. Better that we train a pool of staff for the unit, nurses who already work with babies in the nursery, then we can call on them when we need them. We can do the same with the hospital doctors. Interns on roster in the nursery can do some special-care training, spend two or three days with us so they see the routine.'

'You'll do the training?'

Another smile.

'Let's get the unit up and running first,' she said. She was packing up her papers as she spoke, and added, 'And I really can't do any more until I see the space, so perhaps you'll tell me about the falcons.'

The smile slipped away, and she added quickly, 'Although I have a book to read if you're busy.'

But falcons were his passion, his one diversion from the world of work, so the invitation to talk about them was tempting.

'You know they're hunting birds?'

'Birds of prey, yes,' she said, warm interest in her voice and the sparkle back in her eyes.

'We train them to hunt for us. In days gone by, they provided food for the tribe, but now we hunt for pleasure. Although there are many, many breeds of falcon, we have three main ones we use, the gyr, the saker and the peregrine. We cross-breed them for strength and speed, and in all breeds the female is the bigger and the stronger.'

'I suppose she needs to be to ensure her babies have food,' Liz said, and for the first time he saw her hand rest on her swollen belly.

Perhaps she wasn't as detached as she had appeared...

'They're migratory birds but these days we don't catch and train wild birds visiting our land. They are protected and we have breeding programmes aimed at increasing their numbers. The birds we breed for hunting have passports, much like you and I do, with a photo of the bird and details of its genealogy.'

'To prevent inbreeding?'

It was a natural question, but Khalifa was warmed by her interest.

'Partly,' he admitted, 'but also to prevent theft, and so a lost bird can be returned to her owner, but the main reason is so unscrupulous people can't pass off wild birds as bred ones.'

Now she was frowning.

'Is it such a big business that people would do that?' she asked, and he had to laugh.

'Wait until you see a falcon judging at one of our hunting expos. Every man there thinks he has the best bird. Envy, greed, pride—these qualities are universal, and in our country, no more so than at a falcon judging.'

The laughter made him human, Liz decided. That's why it affected her so much. One minute he was the complete businessman—an aloof, even kingly, businessman, and then he laughed and it wasn't just the fizzing and the sparking, but warmth spread through her, seeping into all the places that had been frozen solid since Bill's death.

Renewing her.

He talked on, about his birds, about watching them

in flight and feeling a surge of freedom as they rose into the air, then the swoop as they sighted prey and plunged back to earth.

'They can travel at three hundred and fifty kilometres an hour,' he said.

'And if they mistime their swoop and hit the ground?'

He laughed again.

'It happens more often than you'd think and, yes, they can be killed or badly injured. In our falcon hospital we have a cabinet with drawers of feathers, so damaged feathers can be replaced, the replacement chosen from hundreds to most closely match the bird's plumage.'

'How do they attach a feather?'

'With a needle and thread, of course.'

Liz found herself laughing, not at the story but with delight that in this strange world to which she travelled was a land where people sewed carefully matched feathers back onto their birds.

Saif broke the merriment, coming in to ask what she would like for whatever meal they happened to be up to now, offering a choice of salads and open sandwiches, small meatballs or arancini. He handed her a menu, pointing out larger meals if she wanted something more substantial but in the end she left the choice to him.

'You are hungry?' Khalifa asked, after Saif had consulted him and departed.

'All the time, it seems,' she admitted, and for a moment Khalifa wondered if she'd say more—blame her pregnancy for her hunger maybe—but once again it seemed the subject was off limits.

Had the father of her baby hurt her in some way?

Could, heaven forbid, the pregnancy have been the result of a rape?

But no matter how it had been conceived, surely once

she'd decided to carry the baby to term, she should have been bonding with it, talking to it, comforting it with touch as well as her voice. He remembered how he'd felt when he'd heard he was to be a father—proud and pleased, a little anxious that he'd prove up to the task, and even though he'd not been as involved as he should have been, a small kernel of excitement and anticipation had come to life within him.

Only to die with his wife and child.

Was this why her attitude towards her unborn child bothered him? Because to him it spoke of a lack of caring, yet in other ways he knew this woman to be extremely empathetic, and very caring.

He longed to know more, yet knew it wasn't his business, and as for the attraction he felt towards her—that was nothing more than a distraction. Saif had set a tray of diverse snacks in front of her, and she was smiling with delight, thanking him for his kindness, sampling things and praising him.

And undoubtedly it *was* jealousy he, Khalifa, was feeling.

What he needed was a parachute.

He pictured flinging himself off the plane and smiled at the stupidity of the thought, but deep inside he knew he'd have to do whatever he could to avoid this woman's company. Yes, they'd have to consult from time to time, but he would throw himself into work, both the work of government and his work as head of the surgical department at the hospital, so there'd be no time for him to be distracted by a flame-haired siren.

A pregnant, flame-haired siren!

CHAPTER FOUR

SAIF took the dishes before asking Liz to prepare for landing, and as the plane dropped lower in the sky and banked, she looked out of the window, seeing a land mass emerging from the clouds, then as the mass became clearer, she made out a long ridge of mountains like a spine running down the curving stretch of land—the land looking golden against the brilliant, blue-green sea that surrounded it.

'Oh,' she cried, as the island took shape. 'It's a dragon!'

Khalifa nodded, his smile one of approval and delight.

'Al Tinine—the dragon,' he said, and Liz felt a shiver of excitement. What might lie ahead in this magical place, this dragon land of myths and legends? A land of deserts and oases, of hunting birds with passports, and an enigmatic man who made her fizz and spark when he laughed?

She watched as the plane dropped lower, seeing now the red harshness of the mountain range, the softer red of desert sands spreading away from it, splotches of green here and there—oases, she imagined—and then a city that from the air looked pink.

Could it really be?

The wheels touched down and the engines roared as it slowed. They were here—in Al Tinine. In Najme, in fact, for Khalifa had told her they'd fly straight to the city where his new hospital awaited her.

Disembarking from the plane was a relief, Liz told herself, yet as she walked down the steps to where a big black four-wheel-drive vehicle waited, she felt a sense of regret.

She and Khalifa hadn't actually become friends, but they'd laughed together once or twice and she'd felt a connection to him—as if some indefinable bond was holding them together.

As wild a thought as the stories of Scheherazade, she told herself, looking around the flat expanse of the airfield and smiling as she noticed not high-rise buildings or even factories on its outer limits but hills of sand.

The Endless Desert—wasn't that what Khalifa had called it?

And suddenly she was excited, looking forward to every minute of this experience, looking forward to being positive and cheerful and, yes, successful in this new venture. She even gave the baby a pat, although getting too attached was still definitely not on—not when Oliver was likely to come out of his coma and want his child.

She'd be its aunt—Oliver couldn't take that away from her—but whether, with Bill gone from his life, Oliver would let her get close to the child, she had no idea.

Neither could she think about it right now for Khalifa, who had exited the plane before her, was talking to the driver of the big vehicle, talking anxiously, then taking out his mobile and pacing back and forth as he spoke to someone.

He glanced towards her, shook his head, then ended the conversation.

'I'm sorry,' he said, moving to stand in front of her, 'but there's an emergency at the hospital and I'm needed there. I would have liked to take you to the palace and see you settled in, but I will have to go directly to the hospital and then my driver will take you from there.'

Palace?

Maybe she'd misheard.

Setting that aside, she hurried to assure him she'd be all right.

'What kind of emergency?' she asked as she slid into the car.

Khalifa was in the front seat and turned to look at her.

'A pregnant woman with a meningioma in the occipital region of her brain. It must be a fast-growing one as the first sign she had was the loss of vision in one eye. Given her condition, we can't use drugs, or radiotherapy so—'

'How pregnant is she?' Liz's brain switched into work mode.

'Thirty-four weeks.'

'And the surgeon needs to get into the back of her skull.' Liz was thinking out loud. 'At thirty-four weeks you could take the baby—give the mother some betamethasone to accelerate foetal lung maturation, then do a Caesar. We can provide care for a thirty-four-week neonate.'

'We?' Khalifa queried, a slight smile lurking on his lips.

'I'll be there. I'll come in with you. What's the point of bringing me all this way to loll around in some palace when a baby might need my help?'

'But you can't— You've just got off a plane.'

'And if you say it's because I'm pregnant I'll probably hit you.' Liz interrupted his faltering arguments. 'This is what I do, Khalifa. And if you're removing a tumour from this poor woman's brain, the last thing she'll need is to wake up and find you've sent her baby off to some hospital miles and miles away.'

Liz hoped she'd made her point, but when Khalifa did respond it was with a question of his own.

'You understand I'll be doing the operation? You

know I'm a surgeon with special interest in tumours of the brain?'

Liz grinned at him.

'Do you really think any woman would go off with a man to a strange country without at least checking him out on the internet?'

He returned her smile.

'You'd be surprised,' he said, 'at how many women would do just that.'

'Not this one,' Liz assured him. 'You'd told me you'd studied medicine, but hadn't talked much about your surgery or said whether you were still practising. I must admit it was reassuring that as a doctor you'd at least understand what is needed in any hospital unit. The fights I've had with bureaucrats who think the setting-up and staffing within a hospital are all about getting the numbers right and meeting something they invariably call the bottom line.'

Khalifa nodded.

'These men exist in my life as well, but at least I have the power to cut off their heads if they annoy me.'

The lurking smile told her he was joking, and she smiled back as she said, 'I'd better remember that, hadn't I? I don't think my head would look too good raised on a pike outside this palace you talk of.'

She hesitated, then, aware she was showing her ignorance or possibly naivety, added, 'Is it really a palace? And, anyway, I don't need to stay with you. Surely there are staff quarters at the hospital.'

His smile broadened and warmth rushed from her curling toes to the top of her head, revealing itself, she was sure, in a rich blush.

'You will stay with me. The place is big enough for dozens of visitors—welcoming strangers and taking them in is part of our culture. And while not a palace in the style of a western fairy-tale, as the home of the ruler, it is called that.'

'But wouldn't the home of the ruler—the real palace—be in the capital?'

The smile turned to laughter.

'Does not the English queen have many palaces? Balmoral and Windsor and who knows what others, as well as the one in London. Now, we will stop talking nonsense about palaces, and you will see Najme as we drive into it.'

It *was* pink! All the buildings not pink stone but pink bricks or pink earth, made perhaps from the local sand—red desert sand. Liz was fascinated, and wanted to ask many questions, but Khlaifa was back into work mode, speaking crisply and confidently on his mobile to someone at the hospital, giving orders for the preparation of a theatre, for a crib, for specialist staff.

In English, Liz realised with a surge of relief. If most of the staff spoke English she wouldn't have to learn Arabic, although as she looked at the flowing script on signs in front of buildings she knew she'd like to learn it—to speak it and to write it.

Another challenge.

One she could forget, she told herself firmly. She probably wouldn't be here long enough to find her way around, let alone learn the language.

Best she should concentrate on work. What could she remember from her early studies about the tumour called a meningioma? Usually benign, she thought, but its growth within the outer covering of the brain—the meninges—could be causing compression on areas of vital function—in this case on the occipital region.

'Has she had any treatment for it?' Liz asked as Khalifa folded his phone and slipped it into his pocket.

'Normally the patient would have been given steroids in an attempt to shrink the tumour, but with her pregnancy it was thought an immediate operation was the best option. We have cribs with radiant heaters at the hospital because we use them to fly at-risk babies to the capital. I've asked one be prepared for you and for staff to be available.'

He paused, turning to look directly at her.

'Are you sure about this?' he asked. 'The journey—you must be tired...'

Liz had to smile.

'When I slept for most of it? Hardly,' she said. 'And isn't this the best way to tackle a new job? To leap right in and find out exactly what you do and don't have on hand? I'm very sorry for the poor woman, but I have to admit I'm excited at the same time.'

She really was, Khalifa realised as he took in the shine in her eyes and the slight flush of colour in her cheeks. He shook his head, unable to believe he'd, just by chance, found a colleague who obviously felt as he did about their profession, felt the physical thrill of a challenge.

Though it was probably best he not think of physical thrills and this woman in the same breath...

'Oh, it's pink as well.'

She whispered the words but he saw wonder in her face and felt a surge of pride because his hospital was truly a beautiful building. Stretched out in a swathe of parkland, the architect had somehow managed, with the design of the multi-level building, to still hint at the shape of the tents his family had used for thousands of years, while the dark pink colour of the walls spoke of desert dunes, the gold highlights desert sunsets.

But all he'd said was, 'We can leave our luggage in the vehicle.'

It was the most unusual hospital Liz had ever seen,

arched openings leading into wide verandas that spread out from every floor, bright rugs and cushions thrown with apparent abandon across the marble tiling. Here and there black-robed women and turbaned men sat around low tables, drinking coffee from tall silver pots set over braziers that looked as if they held live coals.

In a hospital?

'Families like to be close to their loved ones, and this seemed to me a practical way to provide accommodation for them,' Khalifa said, making Liz realise her amazement must be showing.

'And presumably they don't take their cooking fires inside near the oxygen tanks,' she remarked, following him through a self-opening door into the foyer of what looked like a six-star hotel but was obviously the hospital's main entrance.

Voices called what she took to be greetings to Khalifa, some men bowing their heads in his direction, not, she felt, subserviently, but merely an acknowledgement that he was among them again.

He spoke briefly to a woman in loose trousers and a long tunic, a uniform not unlike the clothes Liz had brought with her. *So she'd got that right*, she was thinking when Khalifa took her arm and steered her towards another foyer with a bank of lifts.

This was the bit she still had to get right, she realised as her body reacted with volatile enthusiasm to his touch. She could have lit up an entire fireworks display had the fizz and sparks been visible. It had to be the hormonal shift of being pregnant. She'd put it down to that and, in the meantime, avoid opportunities that involved touch—or smiles, or laughter, or even, if possible, hearing his voice. Toes could only take so much!

'This is the theatre floor,' he said, preparing to lead her

out of the lift, but she dodged his hand and strode ahead then realised she'd turned the wrong way. That was okay. Now she could follow him, trailing in his wake, taking in the ramrod-straight back, the sleek sheen of his hair, and the neat way his trousers hugged—

Totally not going there, Liz!

He led her into a theatre anteroom where a group of men and women were already pulling on hospital gowns over T-shirts and shorts, or were fully gowned and discussing what lay ahead of them.

'This is Dr Elizabeth Jones,' Khalifa announced above the rush of greetings. 'I won't confuse her with all your names at this stage but she'll take care of the baby once it's delivered.'

He beckoned to a woman at one side of the room and she came forward, her dark eyes studying Liz.

'Laya is the head nurse in our nursery,' he explained, and Liz held out her hand.

'Call me Liz,' she said. 'And lead me somewhere I can have a shower and change. Who knows what foreign germs I could be carrying?'

Laya led her into a large bathroom with several shower stalls.

'Theatre gowns are in these cupboards,' she explained. 'I'll wait and get you kitted up.'

Liz grinned at her.

'Kitted up? Is that a local expression?'

'I trained in England,' Laya said. 'I could have chosen the USA but my family had been visiting London for years so I knew people there who were happy for me to live with them.'

She'd been stacking clean theatre gear on a bench so hadn't noticed Liz's baby bump until she turned back towards her.

'Oh!' she said.

'Exactly,' Liz told her, 'though it's not what it seems and, anyway, I'm perfectly well and quite capable of doing my job. Just get me a couple of sizes larger of everything.'

Laya looked as if she'd have liked to protest, or maybe ask more, but Liz hurried into a shower stall, stripping off her underwear then grimacing as she realised she'd have to put it back on again afterwards—or wear some of those enormous paper undies that were available throughout most hospitals. Pity they didn't do large size paper bras.

'Now we're organised,' she finally said to Laya, 'so lead on.'

Scrub up next, then into Theatre, gowned and gloved, where the patient was already on the table, one of the men from the anteroom in place at the patient's head, another man, obviously the obstetrician, preparing for an incision on the woman's swollen belly. Khalifa was on the far side of the room, examining the X-rays and scans on what looked like a flat-screen television fixed to the wall.

Liz checked the preparations Laya had made in the hastily set-up newborn care corner. A trolley of fixed height with radiant warmer, drawers that would hold equipment, an oxygen bottle, a hand-operated neonate resuscitator, scale, pump suction with foot operation, IV cannulas, mucus extractors, soft towels for drying and wrapping the baby, sterile equipment for tying and cutting the cord, feeding tube, sterile gloves—everything seemed to be in place.

As the obstetrician reached into the small incision and drew out the tiny infant, Laya wheeled the trolley close and Liz took the baby—a boy. She used a fine tube to clear his mouth and nose, squeezed his little chest so he began to breathe and then to cry. She held him against his mother's chest, only for a moment, but it felt the right thing to do for both of them, then, when the obstetrician had tied and cut the cord, she set the infant on the trolley and wheeled him to the corner of the room while the surgeons prepared the woman for the next stage of her operation.

'He's come through this well,' she said to Laya, as the vital Apgar numbers added up to six at one minute. She'd used a bag and mask to give him a little extra oxygen, and by five minutes his score was up to nine.

Once dry and warm, they weighed and measured him.

'Fifteen hundred and fifty-eight grams—it's low for thirty-four weeks,' she said to Laya, then glanced over at where Khalifa was preparing to open the woman's skull. 'She possibly hasn't been feeling well for some time, maybe not eating properly. Would she have been seeing a doctor or midwife regularly?'

'I don't know her, but she's from the desert so I doubt it,' Laya said. 'It's all very well to build hospitals and clinics but getting our people, particularly the women, to use them will take a lot longer than His Highness realises.'

'His Highness?' Liz echoed, and Laya nodded towards Khalifa.

'He's our leader—a prince, a highness,' she explained.

Well, that settled all the fizz and sparking stuff, Liz thought, not that she'd ever had any indication that the man might be interested in her. As if he would be, pregnant as she was, and probably not even if she hadn't been pregnant.

A highness, for heaven's sake! And she'd been joking with him!

Though she should have twigged when he'd talked about the palace!

'Did he not tell you?' Laya asked as Liz wrote down the baby's crown-heel length of forty-four centimeteres.

'Well, yes,' Liz admitted, 'but somehow you don't connect a bloke you meet in the corridor at work with royalty. I thought maybe like our prime minister—that kind of leader—an ordinary person with a tough job. Head circumference thirty-three.'

She made another note, her mind now totally on the baby, although the murmur of the surgical teams voices provided a background to all she did.

'I've got a special-care crib waiting. Should we take him to the nursery?' Laya asked when the little boy was safely swaddled and ready to be moved.

Liz glanced over at the woman on the table. The baby's mother was unconscious, of course, but would she have some awareness? Would she know her baby had been taken? Would she need him nearby?

'I think we'll stay here to do the stabilisation,' Liz responded. 'The crib has monitors on it so we can hook him up to them to watch him, and give him anything he needs as he needs it. At this weight he'll probably have some apnoea and will need oxygen support, caffeine to help his lungs...'

She knew she was thinking aloud, but the situation was so strange she wanted to make sure she was ready for every possible problem that could arise. CPAP, the continuous positive airway pressure, could be delivered through a nasal cannula, and if she put in a central venous catheter for drugs and measurements and a peripheral line as well, all the bases would be covered.

But without a special-care unit, where would they take the baby?

To the nursery?

No, from what Khalifa had told her, under normal circumstances they'd fly any premature baby to the capital.

Not a good idea, given what the mother was going through. Liz glanced towards the tall surgeon bent intently over the operating table.

'Do new babies room in with their mothers here at the hospital?' she asked Laya.

'Some do,' Laya told her. 'It's a choice the mothers are offered.'

'And are there on-call staff rooms at the hospital— places where staff can stay over?'

Laya frowned at this question—not a big frown, more a worried grimace.

'Of course. Why are you asking?'

Liz grinned at her.

'I'm thinking maybe *this* baby can room in with his mother,' she said. 'Khalifa—' should she keep calling him that now she knew about the Highness thing? '—said there were few financial restraints and, anyway, it would only mean maybe a couple of shifts of nursery nurses, preferably ones who've worked with fragile newborns, helping stablise them before they're flown out, and we could keep him with the mother. I'd be happy to live in at the hospital to take a couple of shifts, and I'd still be able to do the preliminary work on the new unit at the same time. What do you think?'

It was Laya's turn to glance towards the surgical team.

'I don't know what to think,' she said. 'But once she's out of Recovery, the mother will go into Intensive Care…'

'A very sterile environment for a newborn,' Liz reminded her. 'Of course, we'll have to make sure there's room for the crib and a nurse to watch his monitor, but if there is, wouldn't it be best to have the baby near the mother? Wouldn't that be more of a help to her recovery than a hindrance?'

Laya shook her head.

'I don't know,' she said, glancing again at the table—or more particularly at the lead surgeon, who was still bent over the patient.

'You think he'll be a problem?' Liz teased, then she realised Laya was genuinely distracted.

'I know he lost his wife and child,' Liz said gently, 'but I would have thought that would make him all the more determined to achieve the best outcome for this mother and child.'

'Of course,' Laya told her, 'but...'

'But what?'

Laya hesitated, before saying, in a very quiet voice, 'Will *you* ask him?'

The way she spoke reminded Liz of the fear some surgeons managed to instil in their theatre staff, roaring at the slightest mistake, swearing and cursing when things went wrong. Now she, too, looked back at this particular surgeon. She didn't know him from Adam, but from the time she'd spent with him, she'd have put him down as the very opposite—quiet, reserved, not given to tantrums.

'Is it because of the highness thing you don't want to ask him?' she said to Laya, who looked even more uncertain.

'Not really. But I suppose it must be, because when he was just a doctor, if I did happen to run into him, it was just "Good morning, Doctor" like you do with all the staff you don't know really well. But since he became our leader—well, it changes things, doesn't it?'

Liz adjusted the cannula in the baby's nose.

'Did *he* change?' she asked, and Laya gave the question some thought then shook her head.

'He's not here as often, of course, but when he is he's just the same. And he always knows everyone's name, which most of the doctors and even nurses from other departments don't, but I don't think he's changed. It must be me who's changed.'

'I wouldn't if I were you,' Liz told her. 'Just carry on

as you always did. But, anyway, it was my idea we room the baby with the mother so I'll ask him and make the arrangements, okay?'

Laya's smile told her the nurse had relaxed, and her words delighted Liz even more.

'Will you ask if he can arrange for me to be one of the nurses? I've travelled with preemie babies to the hospital in the capital so I know how to care for them, and I've already put my name down for training in the new unit.'

'Then I'll certainly ask for you,' Liz promised as Khalifa straightened up, stepped back from the patient and pulled off his gloves.

'Clean gown and gloves,' he said to one of the surgical staff, then he walked over to look at the baby, tilting his head to one side as if to take the little being in more clearly.

'You're still here?' He looked up at Liz as he asked the question and though she was about to make a joke about just being a mirage, the strain in his eyes told her this wasn't the time.

'No unit to take him to,' she said lightly. 'And I felt it was important to keep him close to his mother. In fact, Laya and I have just been talking about it, and we'd like him to room in with her if that can be managed. I'd be happy to live in here so I'm always on hand, and Laya and another nurse can share shifts with me. I realise the mother will be in the ICU for a while, but at least the atmosphere will be sterile and when the mother becomes conscious we'll have the baby on hand for her to see so she doesn't feel any anxiety or fear for him. I realise if you're not done there, you can't discuss it now, but we'll wait here until you finish and maybe talk about it then.'

He probably wouldn't understand the slang expression 'stunned mullet' but it described him to a T. Fortunately the scrub nurse called him for his fresh gown and gloves and one of his colleagues needed him back at the table, so any further discussion was suspended.

'He didn't look too happy about your idea,' Laya ventured, and Liz grinned at her.

'That's probably only because he's used to being the one with the big ideas,' she said. 'Once he's had time to think about it, he'll see it makes sense.'

And living in at the hospital would keep her safe from fizzing and sparks—but that was a side benefit. The baby definitely came first.

CHAPTER FIVE

Two hours later, as he stepped away from the operating table, leaving room for one of his assistants to close, Khalifa remembered the baby in the room—the baby and the woman caring for him!

She wanted the baby rooming in with his mother in the ICU?

The idea was bizarre, but even more confusing was her determination to stay at the hospital to care for the newborn. Was her own pregnancy making her ultra-sensitive?

Not that he'd noticed the slightest sensitivity on her part towards her pregnancy—the subject was not open for discussion. Yet it niggled at him, both the pregnancy and her seeming lack of interest in it.

He shoved his soiled gown and gloves into a bin, called for a fresh gown, although he'd finished at the operating table, and eventually, clean again, moved across the room to where the two women waited by the crib.

'The mother will be in Recovery for some time,' he said, addressing the air between Laya and the newcomer. 'I suggest the baby goes to the nursery where Laya can keep an eye on him.'

Now he had to face his new employee. With her richly coloured hair hidden by a cap, the black-rimmed glasses dominated her face, making her skin seem creamier, her eyes a deeper blue.

'Not a good idea,' she said. 'Look at him. You say he's thirty-four weeks, but the mother may have miscalculated. Either that or he's not been well nourished. Put him in among healthy newborns and he'll look more like a skinned rabbit than he already does. Apart from anything else, it would be upsetting for the other mothers, with their chubby little pink-cheeked babies, to see him.'

Khalifa felt a twinge of annoyance. Dr Elizabeth Jones might have seemed the perfect person to set up the new unit at his hospital, but if she was going to argue with him every time he opened his mouth...

'Apart from anything else?' he queried, allowing his voice to reveal the twinge.

'He should be with his mother,' the annoyance replied. 'Not while she's in Recovery, of course, but surely you know where she'll be sent. I can accompany him there and keep an eye on him, and Laya can return to her own shift in the nursery.'

She looked Khalifa in the eye, daring him to argue.

'Minimum fuss, right?' she challenged.

'It is *not* right,' he muttered, glowering at her. 'You've barely arrived in the country, you could be jet-lagged—'

'And might make a mistake?'

Another challenge but before he could meet it she spoke again.

'That's what monitors are for,' she reminded him. 'I fall asleep beside the crib—which, I might add, is highly unlikely—and something goes wrong then bells will ring, whistles will blow and people will come running. I'm a neonatologist, remember, this is what I do. This hospital or Giles, this is my work.'

Again the blue eyes met his, the challenge still ripe in them.

'Any other objections?'

'Wait here!' he ordered, then realised that was a mistake for the baby's mother was already being wheeled into Recovery and the staff beginning to clean away the debris of the operation.

'No, wait outside in the corridor.' He spoke to Laya the second time, avoiding the challenging eyes *and* the disturbing feelings just being near the other woman was causing him. He headed for the changing rooms but once there he realised he should have showered and put on clean clothes on the flight but with Liz—would thinking of her as Dr Jones be better?—in the bedroom he'd not wanted to disturb her.

Now, showered again, changing back into his travel clothes was unappealing and the only apparel he had in his locker was a row of white kandoras and a pile of pristine red and white checked headscarves—kept there for any time he might have to leave the hospital for an official duty.

Not that he minded getting back into his country's clothing. Too long in suits always made him feel edgy, but walking hospital corridors as a sheikh rather than a doctor could be an offputting experience.

He wouldn't wear the headscarf—no, of course he would. Both it and the black cord that held it to his head. He was home!

He was beautiful! Liz could only stare at the apparition that had appeared before her in the corridor. Khalifa and yet not Khalifa, remote somehow in the clothes of his country, a disturbing enigma in a spotless white gown, the twist of black cord around his head covering giving the impression of a crown.

His Highness!

She ran her tongue over suddenly dry lips and tried for levity.

'Good thing it's you, not me, in that gear,' she said. 'White is not a colour for klutzes. I'd have tomato sauce stains down it in no time flat.'

Laya, she noticed, was suddenly busy watching the baby, her head bowed as if Khalifa in his traditional dress had overawed her.

To be honest, he'd overawed Liz as well, but it wouldn't do to show it.

'Follow me,' he said, ignoring her tomato-sauce remark and leading them along the corridor. Laya followed with the crib and Liz brought up the rear, telling herself that staying at the hospital was the best idea she'd ever had. Her body might have behaved badly to Khalifa in civvies, but that was nothing to the rioting going on within it now.

Stupidity, that's what it was.

Hormones.

Oh, how she hoped it was just hormones.

Although, given the impossibility of anything ever coming of her attraction to the man, providing she kept that attraction well hidden it wouldn't matter, would it? Just another unrequited love. She'd survived that once before when her fourteen-year-old self had fallen in love with Mr Smith, the school science teacher. Smith and Jones, she'd written in tiny writing all over the covers of her physics book.

And as she couldn't remember all the elements of Khalifa's name, she couldn't write it anywhere, which was an extremely good thing.

'Here,' a soft voice called, and she turned to find her thoughts had distracted her enough for her to miss the lift foyer so Laya had to beckon her back.

'She's a klutz,' Khalifa was saying to Laya as Liz joined them. 'Do you know that word?'

Laya shook her head and Khalifa proceeded to repeat the explanation Liz had given him in what seemed like another lifetime. She stood there, feeling her cheeks growing hot, uncertain if he was teasing her deliberately or simply passing on something he found of interest to his compatriot. Not that it mattered. While he was talking to Laya he wasn't talking to her and the best thing she could do was avoid all conversations with him.

Fortunately, before she could become too mortified, the lift arrived and they were whisked up to the next level.

From the inside, the ICU looked like any other ICU, although this place was still sparklingly new. But beyond the glass outer walls Liz could see the big arches and the sheltered balconies that must run along the length of the building.

'For the families?' she asked Khalifa, so intrigued her decision to not talk to him was forgotten.

'Of course,' he said. 'Close family members can, as you'd know, come into the ICU for short visits, but the others have to make do with being outside. Most of the time the curtains are open so they can see in, and the patient has the comfort of knowing they are there.'

'So different,' Liz murmured, although the room they were now in could have been in any hospital in the world with its well-positioned monitors, external pacemaker, defibrillator, suction pumps, drains, catheters, feeding tubes and IV lines—a veritable web of tubes that would soon be connected to the baby's mother.

On the other hand, few hospitals would have ICU rooms this big.

'There! In that corner,' she said, pointing to a clear space by the outer window. 'A perfect position for the baby because the mother in the bed will only have to turn her head to see the crib. On the other side, there's just too much gear.'

Laya began to push the crib towards the space Liz had indicated but Khalifa stopped her with a touch of his hand—long, slim fingers—and turned to Liz.

'You're sure about this?' he asked, a slight frown marring the smooth skin on his forehead.

'About the baby rooming in?'

He shook his head, the frown deepening.

'About your own involvement? I could have another neonatal paediatrician here within a couple of hours. You do not have to do this.'

He spaced the words of the last sentence out very carefully, giving each one equal emphasis.

Was it an order in a polite form?

Liz had no idea, she just knew that when the woman woke up, her first thought would be for her baby.

'Quite sure!' Liz, too, spaced her words so he couldn't help but get the message that she was determined to go through with this. 'I'll just need someone to bring my luggage in from the car.'

He shrugged, the white robe lifting on his broad shoulders, the headscarf moving slightly so it showed his face in profile, a stern profile with that long straight nose and determined chin. The lips should have softened it, but they were set in a straight line—not thinned exactly, but straight enough to make Liz wonder if he was far too used to getting his own way.

She smiled at the thought and he caught the smile, raising his eyebrows but actually allowing the line of his lips to relax.

'Do you always get your own way?' he asked, echoing her thoughts so neatly she felt the blood rising to her cheeks once again.

What was wrong with her? This blushing business was totally out of character, and she doubted she could blame it on hormones. After all, she'd got through thirty-plus weeks of pregnancy without blushing when a man teased her...

Not that many men *had* teased her.

Fortunately Khalifa's pager went off with a soft beep and he departed, leaving Laya to wheel the crib into the corner and Liz to collect herself.

'Did you know him before? When you were studying perhaps?' Laya asked, as Liz checked the monitor leads were still attached and the baby seemed comfortable.

'The baby?' Liz joked, although she knew exactly what 'him' Laya had meant.

'No, His Highness,' Laya explained, while Liz wished the nurse would stop calling him that. The words made her, Liz, feel slightly squeamish. 'Did you meet him when he was overseas, training?'

The question was puzzling and although Liz would have liked to ask why, she contented herself with explaining about Khalifa buying the hospital where she worked with the idea of staff interchanges between the two facilities.

'It's a wonderful idea,' she continued, hoping to get Laya's mind off whatever it was she really wanted to know. 'Think what the staff from both countries will learn and how the patients will benefit as a result.'

'But he seems at ease with you,' Laya protested, and it took a moment for Liz to realise she hadn't diverted the other woman at all.

'Oh,' she said, then she conquered the little flash of excitement the simple words had caused and squashed the whole conversation. 'I think he's the kind of man who would be at ease with any woman,' she told Laya. 'Now, we need to gather some supplies for this baby. Can I get you to do that? Do you have special packs on hand for when you airlift babies to the hospital up north? We'll need a couple of them to begin with and a trolley to hold supplies, and scales of course.'

Laya assured her such packs were available and departed, leaving Liz and one very small baby boy in the impressively equipped room. She looked down at the sleeping figure and felt movement from the child she carried.

Her hand moved to touch it—to feel the life within her but she'd been so strong all through the pregnancy, she knew she shouldn't weaken now.

Although with Bill gone, could she not keep this baby?

Selfishness, she told herself. It wasn't hers—it was never going to be hers—that had been the biggest hurdle she'd had to leap when she'd decided to go ahead with the pregnancy. Everyone she knew had warned her of maternal bonds and attachment and she'd been determined it wouldn't happen to her, but now...

To Khalifa's astonishment, the situation with the baby rooming in the ICU seemed to be working. Admittedly, *his* patient had been very groggy when she'd come out of the anaesthetic, but of course Liz Jones had been right—the patient's first thought had been for her baby. In fact, her distress had been so evident that she'd been moved from Recovery to the ICU far more quickly than was usual.

Now, three days later, she lay, as she always did, with her heavily bandaged head turned towards the infant's crib. Only today the crib had been moved closer to his patient's bed and the woman's hand rested on her son's arm, her fingers moving very slowly and gently over his skin.

No need to see who was on duty with the baby. Khalifa

doubted either of the nurses would have orchestrated this arrangement.

Liz nodded at him by way of greeting, as if all this was perfectly normal.

Yet wasn't it?

Mother and baby together—yes, that was normal. But—

'It bothers you?'

Was his confusion so obvious?

'Hospitals have systems and procedures and rules because in that way we can ensure the best outcomes for our patients,' he muttered, grumpy now as well as confused.

The woman had the hide to smile at him.

'And this isn't the best outcome for both our patients?' She nodded towards the pair. 'The two of them linked by the touch of love?'

The touch of love?

Her words struck deep into Khalifa's heart and a sense of loss that had nothing to do with Zara and the baby all but overwhelmed him. Had he ever known it? Certainly not from his mother, who had lived to please one man and one man only, his father. Her children, once born, were cast in among all the other children at the palace, anonymous in the crowd, although his grandmother, his mother's mother, had always sought him out, made him feel special.

Had that been love?

And did Liz know the touch of love, or were they just words? She'd certainly not given any indication that *her* baby had felt that touch.

He shouldn't judge, but her behaviour puzzled him, and now those words.

'You're probably right,' he admitted grudgingly, getting back to the conversation.

'Only probably?' she teased, then she turned the small computer screen so he could see it.

'I can't talk about your patient, but this little chap is doing well,' she said. 'His birth weight fell one hundred and seventy grams but we started feeding him through the orogastric tube on day two—was that only yesterday?—and I hope to have him on full feeds within a week. He's still on the CPAP but we took him off that for an hour this morning and he coped well so we'll gradually wean him off it.'

She was nattering on to him as if he was just another colleague in her life. Which, of course, he was, but...

His mind wanted to follow the 'but' but his instinct warned him not to go where it might lead. Instant attraction was dangerous enough—far too unstable to lead anywhere, in his opinion—but instant attraction to a pregnant woman—that was madness...

'Is she doing well, *your* patient?' the pregnant woman was asking, and he brought his mind firmly back to work.

'Extraordinarily well,' he had to admit. 'Given that she's just had major brain surgery, I actually can't believe how much progress she's made.'

He'd thought his colleague might take advantage of that admission with a smug grin at the very least, but all she did was offer a whole-hearted smile, and a quiet 'I am so glad it's working out for her'.

Some undercurrent in the words made him look at her more closely and he was sure he detected shadows in her lovely eyes.

Shadows of sadness—though how could that be? And why would he think sadness?

Then, on the faintest of sighs, she explained.

'I have a friend in a coma,' she said quietly. 'It's a terrible place to be.'

He wanted to touch her, just a touch of comfort—on her shoulder, or perhaps her arm—but she moved away, clicking off the computer screen, tidying the trolley that held the baby's needs in the corner of the room, although it had looked perfectly tidy when he'd glanced at it earlier.

There'd been something deeply personal in her admission and he couldn't help but wonder if she'd been speaking of the father of her baby.

But in that case, surely she'd be giving the baby *more* reassuring touches, not fewer...

He *had* to get his head straight. He had to stop thinking about the woman, yet how could he when she was here every time he visited his patient?

Every time?

He thought back.

'Have you been getting any rest?' he asked her. 'Are you actually trusting other staff to take care of the baby?'

She looked up from the trolley in the corner and smiled at him.

'Of course I trust the staff and, yes, I'm getting plenty of rest. My body clock is still a bit wonky with the travel, so I come and go at odd hours, and if I'm here I give the nurse on duty a break.'

She made it sound so—*normal*, somehow, yet he knew it wasn't. For one thing, the nearest on-call room was way down the other end of the long corridor.

She must have read his thoughts because she smiled and said, 'And all the walking is the best possible exercise for me.'

He wanted to argue, to tell her she should be living in the palace, but he had no reasons to back up his argument, not one—none!

Yet he wanted her there—he wanted her to see his home, to walk through his gardens, to relax in a hammock beneath the shade of a peach tree...

Though perhaps a klutz in a hammock…and pregnant at that?

On a couch under a peach tree.

'I've seen the area for the new unit.' The shift in conversation startled him. 'And I've drawn up a list of equipment and passed it on to the manager of the children's section of the hospital. Laya tells me the nursery comes under his control so I assumed the new unit would as well. No doubt he'll run the purchases past whoever has to okay them. I'm sure you don't have to be bothered with minor details like that.'

He had to smile.

'I have a niece who uses that phrase—minor details like that—usually when she's spent an inordinate amount of money on some article of clothing.'

To his delight, Liz returned his smile.

'I can assure you I haven't overspent. In fact, I thought we'd start small. No point in having equipment we might never need cluttering up our space, but I have included things like comfortable, reclining armchairs for parents and a plan for the alterations we'll need to the internal space.'

Her smile slipped away, replaced by a slight frown.

'I couldn't cost things like the internal carpentry and plumbing and hadn't a clue who to ask but I'm sure Phil will sort it out. He seems to be on top of everything—fantastic bloke.'

Phil?

Who was Phil?

Of course, Philip Cutler, the young man Khalifa himself had headhunted from a children's hospital in the US to manage the department.

'I'm sure Mr Cutler will manage,' he agreed, aware he sounded stiff and stuffy, but inordinately put out by her seeming friendliness with 'Phil'! She'd only been here a couple of days!

He made a mental note to see the man and check the requirements.

Why? his head asked. Do you not trust one or the other—both—of these staff members?

He didn't answer his head's question because he knew full well his interest was in Dr Liz Jones, not in her lists, but if he kept abreast of her plans then he'd have more to discuss with her, more reasons to see and talk to her.

She is pregnant!

His head was yelling at him now.

She already has a man in her life, or did have within the last nine months!

Yet, for reasons beyond his comprehension, neither issue seemed to affect the attraction he felt towards her, or his—need?—to see her as often as he could, to hear her speak, to make her smile.

Madness!

Had she said something wrong? Liz wondered. Done the wrong thing, giving the list and plans to Phil—somehow made a mistake in this strange situation in which she found herself?

Unease coiled in Liz's stomach as she eyed the man—His Highness—though today he was more a doctor in his civvies, just standing there.

Lost in thought, or just plain lost?

She was lost, so she knew the feeling, but why would this man be feeling lost, here in *his* hospital, in *his* country?

Could it be that he was lost as she was, emotionally?

Of course he would be, she told herself. His wife and child had died. How long would it take to get over such a thing?

For ever?

His state of mind was enough to distract her—just a little—from the usual array of bodily reactions she was experiencing in his presence, although seeing him every day made it easier somehow to cope with—or simply hide—the fizzing and sparks.

'Are you worried about the unit, or is it your patient's condition bothering you?' she asked, to break a silence that had become uncomfortable.

It took a moment but her words must eventually have penetrated his distraction.

'Neither,' he said, then he turned and left the room, not having checked his patient at all, although the ICU doctors were in and out all the time.

It was two days before she saw him again, and this time he whisked into the room with enough purpose in his stride for her to guess this was a medical visit and nothing more. He was also in full highness uniform of white gown and headscarf, so imposing her breathing stilled, faltered, and hitched somewhere in her chest before she pulled herself together.

She concentrated on the baby, in the corner this morning while she changed his feeding tube, and forced herself to breathe normally—to ignore the man in the white gown and folded red and white checked headscarf.

Although hadn't she wanted to talk to him about something?

Something that had been worrying her?

Work, brain, work! she ordered.

What had it been?

Oh, well, if she couldn't remember, surely it hadn't been important enough to bother him with it.

Or had it?

Before she'd sorted out an answer to that question, he'd finished with his patient and was gone.

And, of course, she'd remembered her concern.

She pressed the little bell that would summon the nurse on duty from the tea room and when Laya appeared, left her in charge of the baby, hurrying down the corridor to catch Khalifa.

'There *was* something I wanted to talk to you about,' she said, coming up behind him and touching him lightly on the shoulder.

He turned abruptly, as if her touch had stung him, and she wondered, briefly, if one shouldn't touch a highness. Then her concern for her patient's wellbeing swept that worry aside.

'The woman, the baby's mother, she's not had family visiting, or anyone outside on the veranda. Laya said she was from the south and you spoke of an Endless Desert. Do you think perhaps her family don't know they can visit—or maybe they don't know she and the baby are here? Has anyone tried to contact them? I don't know the protocol, of course, but I walk around the other wards and see the families by the windows and I love the idea of such support for the patients, but our little mother and her baby seem to have no one.'

Khalifa just stared at her, and again she wondered if she'd done the wrong thing—spoken out of turn, interfered where she shouldn't.

But when he spoke it was against himself, not her.

'Have you bewitched me in some way that not only do I allow you to rearrange the ICU to suit your ideas but I've let slide my concentration on my own patient? Of course her family should be somewhere near her, although...'

He looked concerned and she'd have liked to touch him again—a comforting pat on the arm, nothing more...

Instead, she prompted him.

'Although?'

'She *is* from the desert, from one of the tribes who are finding the new ways more difficult to accept. The fact that the family aren't here tells me we haven't made it clear enough that they are free to come and go, to visit when they wish, and remain within their family group on the veranda. We're not getting the message across that although the buildings are different, our customs can remain intact.'

'I'm sure you will,' Liz told him, and she meant it because the more she saw and heard of this man, the more she understood his deep, abiding love for his land and his people, and his concern for every one of them.

Khalifa knew it wasn't an empty assurance. She really meant it, as if she already knew him in ways even friends might not fathom.

The thought was so strange it took him a moment to process it, then he dismissed it as some fantasy that was part of whatever happened to his brain whenever he was around this woman.

Though his brain's reaction wasn't nearly as bad as his body's. Two days since he'd seen her, and one glimpse in that ICU room had had his body hardening, heating, burning…

Escape had been the only answer, although, now she'd caught up with him, hadn't he come to the hospital this morning to tell *her* something?

Of course, the paediatrician!

'On the subject of *your* patient,' he began, reverting to head of the hospital, even head of the country mode, 'I should have told you earlier. A trained neonatal paediatrician will be here…' he checked his watch '…within the next hour. She's flying down from Al Jabaya and will take over the care of the baby here at the hospital.'

Liz Jones turned towards him, her eyes narrowing slightly.

'You're sacking me?'

The question was asked lightly, but it was not quite a tease.

'Just freeing you up to do the work I brought you here to do,' he replied, equally lightly—he hoped! 'You will be welcome to visit the baby, of course, and I know you'll want to talk to Dr Hassan when she arrives, but this afternoon a driver will collect you and your luggage and drive you out to the palace. Four o'clock at the main entrance? That would suit you?'

She wanted to argue—he could see it in the stiffening of her body and the flash of some emotion in her eyes. Not anger, he thought, perhaps offence at his attitude. A dislike of taking orders? He had no idea, but once again, when he knew full well he should be distancing himself from her, the woman had intrigued him to the extent that he was making guesses at her reactions.

Enough!

Anyway, she'd relaxed again, her face now blandly composed.

'Four o'clock at the front entrance,' she repeated, and he sensed she'd have liked to snap a salute. 'I'll make sure I'm there.'

CHAPTER SIX

OF COURSE *he* was waiting for her. Yes, a driver would have been far more sensible, but where this woman was concerned he seemed to have lost touch with what was sensible. No matter how much he told himself there was other work to do, that there were things he shouldn't be putting off, he couldn't overcome his urge to see her reaction to his city, to the drive to his home, to his home itself.

'Is this chauffeuring a part-time job, something you do for extra cash when you're not being a highness?' she teased as he took her bag from her hand and tossed it in the back seat of the big, black, four-wheel drive vehicle.

'I was going home anyway,' he said, not quite a lie as he could work from the palace. But the 'highness' jab had struck home.

'Highness is nothing more than a title, like Mr or Dr,' he told her. 'It was never used in our country until recently when the paparazzi began to shove it in front of our names. Now suddenly every tribal leader in the region is His Royal Highness, as if we're European royalty. The problem is, our people are picking up on it as well.'

He glanced towards his passenger.

'Does it bother you?'

But apparently she didn't hear the question, for as he'd asked it she'd turned to look out the window. The moment coincided with his driving out of the hospital gates and they were passing a new souk that had sprung up at the entrance to the new building, market stalls appearing almost overnight, selling everything from herbs and spices to women's underwear.

'Oh, the colour! I didn't see this as we drove in,' his passenger murmured. 'Can we stop? May I get out and have a look?'

He pulled over on the other side of the road, tossing up in his mind whether to stay in the car, knowing there'd be deference if he walked through the market yet wanting to share the experience with her.

The latter won and he slipped out of the car, coming around to take her arm as she clambered awkwardly down from the high seat.

She breathed deeply, taking in the many different aromas of the market, smiling already, although they hadn't entered any of the narrow pathways between the stalls.

'What is the smell?' she asked, turning to him, the delight in her smile causing havoc in his chest.

'Spices, rosewater, incense, coffee, lemons—a mix of all those and probably a dozen other things,' he told her, keeping his hand on her elbow and guiding her across the road, nodding to people who greeted him but concentrating on keeping her steady on the rough, stony ground.

'Oh, look at that—pyramids of colour. How do they do that? What is it?'

She'd stopped only metres down the first alleyway where tall cones of gold and russet and green and black drew the eye.

'This is the spice seller,' he explained. 'Spices and herbs.'

He pointed to the drying herbs hanging in bunches from the supports that held the sheltering tent upright.

'So, tell me what the spices are,' she demanded, moving closer, her hands not quite touching the solidly built cones of spices.

The fact that she assumed he knew which spice was which amused him. Names of spices? He knew the tastes but...

Asking the stallholder, he translated.

'The deep red is paprika, the yellow is tumeric, the greenish-grey is cumin and the black, of course, is pepper. In the big glass jar, saffron threads—see.'

The stallholder had pulled some threads of saffron from the jar and handed them to Khalifa.

He pressed them into Liz's hand, feeling the softness of her skin—

'But such huge stacks of it when all you use is a pinch,' Liz said, sniffing at the saffron, half turning towards him so the softness her breast was pressed against his hand and the havoc in his body strengthened to chaos.

'I think they do it to attract attention to the stall,' he said, hoping the prosaic reply had hidden his reaction to her closeness.

'Well, that works!' she said, smiling at him in such a natural way he wanted to stay right here, holding her arm, surrounded by the noise and scents and bustle of the souk, possibly for ever.

But she'd plunged on, finding a tall, silver coffee pot and holding it up, turning it this way and that to catch the few rays of the sun penetrating the narrow passage between stalls.

'It's a design from the south,' he said, pointing to a triangular symbol etched on the side. 'That's one of the tattoos the desert women might have worn to ward off evil spirits.'

She put the pot down, serious now.

'I forgot to ask you. What happened with the relatives of your patient? Did you get in touch with them?'

'My grandmother has gone down to visit them. She will tell them what has happened and bring back as many of the relatives as wish to come.'

'Your grandmother? You still have a grandmother? You *are* lucky!'

He had no doubt that she meant it, and remembered now her telling him of her parents' deaths then her brother being killed.

'You have no living relatives?' he asked, and she shook her head, then she smiled and for the first time that he could remember, right there in the colour and clamour of the souk, she patted the bulge of her stomach.

'Well, I suppose you could say this one will be a relative—a niece or nephew. We'd thought later…'

Liz felt the tears sting her eyes and couldn't believe this was happening to her. Right here, in a marketplace, in a strange country, with a strange man, she was about to give in to the tears she'd held back for so long.

And that she *was* going to give in to them she had no doubt, for they were welling up inside her like a wave about to crash onto the shore.

'Let's get out of here,' she gabbled at her host, and without waiting for his reply she plunged back the way they'd come, past the silver coffee pot and the pyramids of spices, heading blindly for the big black vehicle, thankful it had tinted windows so her feeble-minded collapse wouldn't be witnessed by the crowds of people entering and leaving the marketplace.

Khalifa put his arm around her, sheltering her from the crush, feeling the tension in her muscles as she drove forward, helping her into the car, closing the door, and quickly starting the car. Just down the road and off to the left was a small oasis, rarely visited as most people preferred the big parks in the centre of the city.

It was a beautiful place, where the red desert sands met the soft green of the tiny area, the sand hills slowly moving closer to the water but the vegetation fighting back.

He took her there, aware that some emotion was tearing her apart, helpless to help her as she held her hands to her face, unable to stop the tears that streamed between her fingers or the sobs she muffled with her fists.

But once he'd stopped in the shade of a squat date palm, he could put his arm around her and draw her close to his body, hoping human contact might be of comfort.

Holding her, was, of course, a huge mistake on his part, for this close he could smell the fragrance of her hair, the scent of her body, feel the softness of her flesh, the rise and fall of her breasts as she struggled to regain her composure. He stroked her arm—her skin silky smooth, lightly tanned, with fine, sun-kissed golden hairs that flirted with his fingertips.

And *his* flesh, weak as it was, delighted in all of this; *his* skin heated—that thin line between attraction and lust dangerously close.

Thankfully, she moved, just slightly, in his arms, then pushed away, her glasses dropping onto the floor of the car, her hands rubbing furiously at her face, dashing away remaining tears, reddening her cheeks, tousling her hair, so when she turned to him she could only shake her head.

'I'm sorry, I truly am! I had no idea all that emotion was going to come pouring out! I didn't even know it was in there! And, believe me, I don't do tears—not like that. Blame the hormones.'

She was acutely embarrassed and angry with herself as well, that much was clear to see, but...

'I don't think there's anything to be ashamed of in emotion,' he said quietly. 'We all feel it, so can't we be allowed to show it?'

He won a smile—not the reaction he'd expected but one he enjoyed nonetheless.

'Do you?' she teased, and he must have looked bemused because she clarified the question for him. 'Show emotion?'

'Me?' he said, but he had to smile, teasing her back. 'But I'm a highness, remember. It wouldn't do for me to be weeping all over the place.'

He touched her lightly on the cheek.

'Seriously, though, those tears probably needed to come out, hormones or not. It's all very well to carry on working as if nothing has happened in your life, but losing your brother, your last living relative, that must have brought terrible pain.'

She turned away from him—from his touch?—and...

A memory stirred, a recent memory that had been lost in *his* emotional reaction to holding her in his arms.

'You said the child...'

How to put it?

'The child you're carrying—a relation—a niece or nephew? It's not your child?'

For a moment he thought she was going to ignore him, then she rested her hands on the bulge of her belly, smoothing the material of her tunic over it.

Hesitating...

Debating whether to tell him something.

'The baby is Bill and Oliver's,' she said quietly. 'I think I told you how they saved my sanity and kept me going when our parents died. They were my only family, and I loved them both. For years they'd talked of having a child, of getting a donor egg, finding a woman willing to be a surrogate, but every time they discussed it with me—Bill was a lawyer and Oliver's in finance so I was the best person to talk to about it—I felt this twinge deep inside me. It took me a while to figure it out, but in the end I knew it was something I could do for them—that I *wanted* to do for them.'

'To carry their child?'

She looked up at him, her eyes clear now, and smiled, a smile so full of loving memories he felt his heart tear.

'It made sense, you see. Using my egg would be as close to Bill's DNA as we could get, so Oliver donated sperm and that was it.'

'You make it sound so normal, but carrying someone else's child? Giving over nine months of your life to provide your brother and his partner with a baby? Was it legal? And personally did it not bother you in the slightest? Did it not bother the two men that you wanted to do it?'

She shook her head, the dark red hair, which had come out of its knot as she'd cried, now tumbling about her shoulders.

'The legal side was okay. Surrogacy is legal as long as it's not for profit. And of course it bothered Bill and Oliver, especially when the bloke I was going out with at the time was so horrified he dropped me like a hot potato. But once they knew I was serious, they were delighted, and just so excited. They made me see a counsellor first, and they discussed it with the same psychologist, but eventually it all fell into place.'

Liz smiled as she remembered the joyous delight of that time—a sad smile maybe, but the pair had been beside themselves.

'They went nuts,' she told Khalifa. 'They made recordings of their voices singing lullabies and talking—recordings I could play to the baby day or night, always changing them, telling the baby things about their lives and the lives all three would have together.'

'And you? Where we you in all of this?'

He sounded stern, almost angry.

She met his gaze, knowing other people had found the decision hard to accept but wanting this man to understand.

'I did it willingly. It was my idea to carry their child— you have to believe that. Oh, I knew the dangers. I knew I couldn't get too emotionally attached to the baby, but Bill and Oliver were so besotted that was easy.'

'Until the accident?'

Emotion closed her throat again but she was *not* going to cry! Not again!

Instead she nodded.

'Bill was killed, Oliver is in a coma, and the poor baby is in limbo.'

'But surely now you'll keep him or her,' Khalifa protested.

Liz sighed.

'You'd think it would be that easy, wouldn't you? But, in fact, if Oliver comes out of the coma, and if he still wants the baby, really it's his.' She tried for a smile but knew it hadn't worked too well when Khalifa reached out and drew her close again, holding her against his body, stirring *her* body so heat moved in places she hadn't known existed and tremors of excitement not only fizzed but bounded along her nerves.

She wanted to snuggle closer, to bury herself in him— not an easy task given the size she was—but to lose herself in sensation for just a short time would be so blissful, so soul-restoring. She snuggled just a little bit...

* * *

SAVE UP TO 25%

Subscribe to Medical today and get 5 stories a month
delivered to your door for 3, 6 or 12 months and gain
up to 25% OFF! That's a fantastic saving of over £40!

MONTHS	FULL PRICE	YOUR PRICE	SAVIN
3	£43.41	£36.90	**15%**
6	£86.82	£69.48	**20%**
12	£173.64	£130.20	**25%**

As a welcome gift we will also
send you a FREE L'Occitane
gift set worth £10

**PLUS, by becoming a member you
will also receive these additional benefits:**

🌹 FREE Home Delivery

🌹 Receive new titles TWO MONTHS AHEAD of the shops

🌹 Exclusive Special Offers & Monthly Newsletter

🌹 Special Rewards Programme

No Obligation - You can cancel your subscription at any time by writing
to us at Mills & Boon Book Club, PO Box 676, Richmond. TW9 1WU.

To subscribe, visit
millsandboon.co.uk/subscriptions

The kiss began as nothing. All he did was hold her close
to comfort her, then press his lips against a bit of skin that
was right there beside them. The pale bit near her temple
where a pulse fluttered as his lips touched it.

How it became a lip kiss he later couldn't work out, but
lips *had* certainly been involved and awkward as it had
been in the front of a vehicle, with a very pregnant woman,
it had galvanised his body in a way he'd never felt before.

She tasted of peach and honey and warmth and woman,
her lips opening to him, her breath coming in little gasps
that tightened his body even more. His hands found her
breasts, and a tiny moan escaped her lips, catching on his
tongue—igniting him.

A thousand reasons not to be here—not to be doing
this—were thundering in his head, but nothing mattered
except the kiss…and holding her and having her kiss him,
feeling her hot, soft body up against his, tasting the honey
and the peaches and the woman…

He supposed it had to end, yet he felt distinctly put out
when she drew away, rubbing her hands across her face
then turning to look at him.

'Oh, I'm sorry!' she cried. 'Oh for heaven's sake! I can't
believe I did that!'

He was assuming she meant the kiss, but when she
pulled a handkerchief from her handbag and reached out
towards him, he realised the kiss, apparently, had meant
nothing more than comfort and her distress was the result
of something quite different.

As she rubbed ineffectually at a bright yellow streak
of saffron across his kandora, he wasn't sure whether to
be offended or amused.

'It doesn't matter,' he told her, taking her hand and closing it gently over the handkerchief.

She looked at him now, at his face—met his eyes, her

own seeming naked, defenceless, without the terrible glasses.

'None of it?' she asked.

'Ah!' he said. 'As to that, I don't know! Can you deny the attraction between us?'

A shake of her head, a grimace, then she sighed.

'At least I can blame my hormones being out of kilter,' she said, attempting a smile so valiant it made his toes curl. 'What's your excuse?'

And when he didn't answer—how could he when he didn't know?—she spoke again.

'And what's even more bizarre is how you could possibly be attracted to so hugely pregnant a woman? Is it a kinky thing?'

He laughed and reached out to push the hair back off her face.

'I've no idea,' he told her, knowing she deserved honesty. 'Though I can tell you I've seen my fair share of pregnant women and it's never happened to me before.'

'Which is probably a good thing,' Liz replied, the sternness in her voice belied by the smile with which she said the words. 'So let's put it down to an aberration and ignore it,' she suggested. 'I've got a job to do and from all I hear you've got about a hundred different duties on top of your hospital work, so we've really no time for a dalliance.'

'Dalliance?' he echoed, not knowing the word.

'A little fling—a flirtation—that kind of thing,' she told him.

'Ah,' he said again, and wondered just what else there was to say.

Not that she gave him a chance.

'It was just a kiss,' she said, setting her glasses firmly back in place. 'Let's not make too much of it. Now you know where I am at the moment, you'll understand I don't need any further complications. I'm here to do a job and I'll do it. I'll get the unit going for you then return home to have this baby and sort out something for it. Honestly, Khalifa, that's about all I can cope with at the moment.'

He heard truth in her words—heart-rending truth—and marvelled that she'd coped as well as she had up to now. He wanted to tell her how much he admired her, and offer any help within his power, but she'd obviously decided the conversation was finished for she was clambering out of the car then steadying herself on the door as she slid off her sandals.

'Do you realise this is the first bit of desert I've seen since the plane landed and I saw sand hills in the distance? I want to feel the sand, to see if it's as soft as it looks.'

She stepped away from the car, squishing her feet in the sand, then bent to take a handful and let it fall like water from her fingers.

'It is!' she called to him, her delight so obvious he had to smile.

And had to join her as she climbed the hill. He took her hand as it grew steeper and hauled her up to the top.

They sat together, not too close but close enough that he knew she could feel his warmth as he felt hers. Not far away a random gust of wind stirred the sand into an eddy.

'There's a sand sprite,' he said, pointing to it.

'We'd call it a whirly-whirly,' she said, as the lifting twirl of sand danced across the surface of the dune.

'But are your whirly-whirlies real?' Khalifa asked her.

'Real?'

He nodded, smiling at her surprise.

'My people believe the sand sprites are good spirits— a little like djinns but less mischievous. There's a story of a sand sprite we tell the children.'

Liz lay back in the sand, so at ease with this man she

barely knew, so delighted to be in this strange place, she wanted the moment to go on and on.

'Tell me?'

He smiled at her, then relaxed, easing back on to one elbow so he could watch her face as he talked.

'The legend tells us that once, long ago, there was a sand sprite who had magical powers. At night she turned into a beautiful woman, and she went about the land, fixing things that the djinns had interfered with, making things right for people, helping them.'

He paused then added, 'Not unlike a certain Australian doctor in that way.'

'I've been doing my job, nothing more. Just get on with the story.' She was embarrassed by his words but not as embarrassed as she felt every time she saw the smear of yellow across his white gown, or thought of how she'd reacted to his kiss.

'Well, one night she met a prince who was so handsome and dashing she couldn't help but fall in love with him, so now, every night, instead of doing good deeds she sought out the prince and spent her time as a human kissing him.'

'Which just shows the danger of kisses,' Liz put in, only half joking.

'It does,' Khalifa agreed very solemnly, 'for kisses led to other things and in the end they spent a night making love, but what the sand sprite didn't realise was that once she'd made love with a human, she couldn't go back to being a sand sprite ever again and had to stay as a human for ever.'

'They made love? This is a children's story?' Liz queried.

Khalifa grinned at her.

'In the children's version they get married.'

'But if it's told as a cautionary tale, what's the catch?

Did they not live happily ever after? Did she prefer being a sand sprite to being human and pine away and die? Did the djinns take over the world, without her to undo their mischief?'

'I'm not entirely sure,' Khalifa admitted. 'My grand-mother told me the story and her stories usually carried a warning of some kind. "Be good or the djinns will get you" was the most common.'

'Perhaps the story was more for girls,' Liz offered. 'A warning about the dangers of kissing handsome princes.'

She sat up and dusted the sand off her hands, then gasped in wonder as she turned and caught the full beauty of a desert sunset. Above the sea of dunes, the sky was aglow with orange fire, streaks of red along the horizon and paler gold melting into the dark blue of the evening sky.

'I hope she came to life in time to see this every eve-ning,' Liz whispered, reaching out to rest her hand on Khalifa's because she had to share the beauty and the won-der of it, for all she knew touching him was dangerous.

'I'm sure she did,' he told her.

They sat in silence, hand in hand, until the colours faded from the sky, then he helped her to her feet and steadied her as they clambered down the sand hill and back to the vehicle.

'Thank you,' she said, when she'd fastened her seat belt and he was about to shut the door. 'Thank you for giving me comfort when I needed it, for telling me the story, and most of all for sharing the beauty of that sunset with me.'

He touched her lightly on the cheek.

'It was my pleasure,' he said, and for some obscure rea-son the words made her feel sad again, as if something wonderful had ended when, in fact, there was so much still ahead. The palace, and seeing more of this magical country, and then there was her job—setting up the new unit—a challenge she'd been looking forward to.

So maybe the sadness was hunger.

She was silent as he drove back to the main road, silent as they passed through the outskirts of the city, where streetlights were coming on and the dusk masked any difference she might have noticed in daylight. But as they approached the palace Khalifa watched her turning this way and that as if the rammed-earth walls of what had been an old fort needed to be viewed from many different angles.

'This is your palace?'

'Close,' he told her. 'The fort was built in ancient times. See the turrets there along the western wall? They were the lookouts for the enemies.'

'Did enemies only come from the west?'

'Foreign enemies,' he admitted. 'Though there were plenty of fights between the tribes themselves but that was more a sport—which team would win the competition this year, that kind of thing. When foreign enemies came, all the teams—the tribes—joined together.'

The vast wooden gate into the fort swung open as the car approached, the two men who had lived to open the doors now replaced by an automatic opening mechanism. Although the two men still sat, one of either side of the door, rising to their feet and saluting as he drove in.

'Oh!'

A small sound, but enough to delight him, for it told him Liz had been startled by the beauty of the courtyard that lay behind the walls. Formally laid out with a sparkling fountain in the centre, it held fruit trees as well as ornamental plants, and gardens filled with roses, all now in full bloom.

'It's unbelievable,' she said. 'To see such beauty when

all around is dry and barren. Of course the desert is beautiful, too, in its own way, but this is lovely.'

She shook her head and Khalifa was filled with absurd happiness at her appreciation.

'Has it always been this way?' she asked, as he pulled up at the bottom of a shallow flight of steps that led up to the veranda in front of the guest quarters.

'Always,' he said. 'I think I told you Najme was built on an oasis. Many centuries ago the caliph—that is our term for highness—ordered water to be channelled underground so the garden would always be green. And although the gates are kept closed at night, by day anyone can enter the courtyard and rest in the garden. Children can splash in the fountain and their mothers can pick fruit. The rule is you take only what you and your family will eat that day, so there is always plenty for everyone.'

'And that happens? People take only what they need?'

'Of course,' he said, but in his head he was putting the words into another context, remembering the kiss, certain from her reaction that she'd taken only what she'd needed—comfort—from it. Then she'd warned him off. Put it down as an aberration, she'd said.

Which was just as well, given his track record with pregnant women! An image of Zara popped obligingly into his head and he knew with total certainty that nothing must come of the attraction.

CHAPTER SEVEN

LIZ was still gazing around at the lush colour of the courtyard, unable to believe such beauty had been hidden behind the dull red walls of the fort. Khalifa opened the door and helped her down from the car and his touch on her arm not only brought the usual reactions but with them a determination to ignore all physical manifestations of this attraction and to steer clear of this man whenever possible. She would treat him as her boss, nothing more—no chats or teasing or bleating out her problems...

He led the way up shallow steps and kicked off his sandals at the front door. She stared at the jumbled collection of sandals already there and forgot her good intentions, reaching out to hold his shoulder as she slid her own sandals off, asking, at the same time, 'This is a guest house? Do you have so many guests? There must be more than a dozen pairs of sandals lined up there.'

He steadied her then bent to add her sandals to the rather ragged line, then pointed out the small pairs.

'Four children, I would say, although my grandmother has tiny feet so if she's back from the Endless Desert one pair could be hers. Then the...'

He paused, frowning, and Liz wondered if he recognised one pair in particular, but when he continued, she realised he'd been working out how to explain.

'We have young women who look after the house and cook and mind the children. They are not exactly servants for they are usually related—members of our tribe—and their families live here with them so all the children grow up together. My child, if she had lived, would have grown up with the other children, and everyone who is in the house for a meal sits down together for it—all the women and children.'

It sounded very democratic, yet Liz had to ask.

'And the men?'

'In the past, when we were nomadic and our people roamed the desert, the men ate together by the fire outside the tent. This was to guard the women and the children inside. They could also discuss the days ahead, plan hunting trips or forays into foreign territories. Now the men talk politics, which is probably the same thing, but many men now eat with their wives and children—the evening meal at least. Many of the family now live in Al Jabaya, so you'll find mainly older family members here and the young women who look after them.'

He was leading the way into a wide vestibule as he spoke and Liz followed, although her mind had snagged on the image of the fire outside the big tent, the men around it, cleaning guns perhaps, guarding their women and children.

'Khalifa!'

The first child who appeared was a very small girl who raced towards Liz's boss and threw herself into his arms. Other children followed, then a couple of older women, three young women, heads demurely covered with bright scarves, but their faces alight with happiness at seeing the man she was with.

'This is Dr Jones,' he said to the gathering crowd. 'I

would introduce you all, but learning too many names at once will confuse her. Who will be taking care of her?'

A young woman in a blue headscarf stepped forward.

'It will be my pleasure,' she said, in prettily accented English. 'I am Mori.'

'And I am Liz,' Liz told her, stepping forward and holding out her hand.

Mori took it shyly and gently squeezed Liz's fingers then said, 'If you would like to come this way, you can rest before dinner.'

Liz began to follow, then realised she hadn't thanked Khalifa for bringing her here. But when she turned he'd moved away and was deep in conversation with an older woman in black. The woman's hand was resting on his arm, and from the way he looked at her—with love, Liz thought—it had to be his grandmother.

She wanted to ask if the baby's mother's relations had been found, but Mori was moving further away and one glance down the seemingly endless corridor off the vestibule told Liz if she didn't follow she might be lost for ever.

The room Mori showed her into was bigger than her entire flat back home, the *en suite* bathroom the size of her living room. The floor was tiled in what looked like marble, the walls the dark pinkish red she'd seen on buildings in the city, but they were striped with horizontal bands of gold that matched the elaborate patterns woven in gold thread in the curtains around the bed, and the gold and red embroidery on the thick carpet beneath her feet.

'This is beautiful,' she breathed. 'All the colours of the sunset over the desert dunes.'

'Khalifa calls it the sunset room. When he rebuilt the palace so he'd have a home in Najme he named all the guest rooms.'

Did he, now? Liz thought, pleased with this tiny

glimpse into a sentimental part of the man she was only beginning to know.

Beginning and ending, she told herself. He'd comforted her when she'd needed it, and comfort had led to a kiss, but her life was already swamped in confusion, and she had no intention of making it even more convoluted by giving in to her attraction to the man.

She opened her small bag and realised that just about everything in it was dirty. She'd gone through all but one of the outfits she'd brought with her. This last she'd shoved in on the off chance she might have to get dressed up some time—a long, floaty dress in different shades of blue. Holding it up, she wondered whether it was appropriate, but Mori, looking at it, assured her it was beautiful and that most of the women dressed up for dinner.

'I will take your other clothes and wash them, and if you need something else to wear, the cupboards in the dressing room have a selection of clothes in different sizes, all of them new.'

'Why is that?' Liz asked, intrigued by a guest room that came complete with clothing for the guest.

'In other times, people who had nothing would be taken in by the tribe. In the desert you cannot turn strangers away, for on their own they would surely die. If a person is hungry you must feed him or without clothes then you must cover him. That is our way.'

And when a person needs comfort, you comfort her, Liz added to herself just to make sure she understood that the attraction was going nowhere.

Once showered and dressed, she followed Mori to a huge room where women were already seated around a long piece of woven material stretched out on the floor. It would have been a tablecloth, Liz realised, had there been a table.

She joined Mori on a cushion on the floor.

'This is Rimmi, Khalifa's grandmother.' Mori introduced her to the small woman on the other side of Liz. 'She is the head of the house and likes to keep to the old ways, which is why we eat like this for breakfast and for dinner, everyone together.'

Mori rattled off a conversation Liz couldn't understand, but it must have been an introduction for the older woman, Rimmi, turned and took Liz's hand, squeezing her fingers gently and smiling with a warmth that had Liz immediately smiling back.

'Could you ask her if she has been down into the desert and found the relatives of the woman in hospital?' Liz asked Mori, who spoke again.

Rimmi's grasp tightened on Liz's fingers and she nodded then spoke, her voice a husky whisper.

'She says the family is already at the hospital and you are to be thanked and most blessed for all you have done.'

Liz smiled at the compliment and thanked Rimmi, then glanced up, startled, as an excited chatter spread among the women, while the children were positively yelping with glee.

As was Liz's stupid heart, for Khalifa had entered the big room and apparently intended to share the meal with the women and children.

She watched the reactions around the table as he bent and kissed the women one by one, tousling the hair of the little ones he passed before settling down on the other side of his grandmother.

Liz told her racing heart to stop its nonsense, and nodded to the man. She longed to ask Mori about his presence, but obviously she couldn't with him sitting so close.

And so at ease! His long body settled comfortably on the cushion, his legs hidden beneath a clean white gown,

the sides of his headscarf tucked up tonight in some com-
plicated fashion so she could see more of his face than
was usually revealed when he wore his traditional dress.

Such a strong face. Having heard his stories of the men
around the campfire, she could picture him in olden times,
a rifle slung across his lap, perhaps a child held against
his shoulder, for this man, she guessed, could be both
hard and soft.

Now food appeared, great bowls of it, the steam rising from the bowls carrying all the scents of the market
they'd visited earlier, deliciously woven into mouth-wa-
tering dishes.

Rimmi served Liz, Khalifa explaining what each
spoonful was as it was placed on her plate. He passed her
bread to eat with it, then demonstrated on his own plate
how to use it to scoop the food to his mouth.

'Although there is cutlery if you'd prefer. You'll find it
wrapped in that napkin in front of your plate.'

Liz grinned at him and picked up the napkin.

'Better safe than sorry,' she said.

And was surprised when he murmured, 'Klutz,' very
softly but with an undertone of affection that caught her
off guard so for a moment she forgot about keeping her
distance from him and smiled.

He'd known he shouldn't come— should have eaten at his
own house—but all his brothers and their families were
up in the capital, and he'd felt like company.

Felt like Liz Jones's company, the last functioning cell
in his brain had whispered, and he'd been unable to deny it.

Fortunately, before he could become too entangled in
his thoughts, Rimmi demanded his attention, talking to
him but apparently meaning the conversation to include
Liz Jones as well, for she had asked Mori to translate.

'The people of the desert—the people I spoke to—do not understand the hospital,' she was saying. 'To them it is a place where people die, so they do not wish to go there. Somehow you must explain better, to the women in particular, that going to the hospital, or to one of the clinics in the oasis villages, is the best thing to do for themselves and their children.'

'And the men?' Khalifa asked.

Rimmi shrugged her shoulders.

'Ah,' she said, 'the men! As good to talk to the camels or the date palms. But you must talk to the women. Take Dr Jones with you so they see it is a woman they will deal with, and let her explain about what can be done when pregnancy or births go wrong. A woman can tell other women.'

Khalifa glanced at Liz. Had she taken it all in? Had Mori translated it properly?

She smiled at him and nodded as if he'd asked the questions aloud, and her eyes sparkled as she said, 'You and I talked about doing this earlier—was it on the plane or before that? I can't remember. Talked about taking a crib and explaining what happens in a special-care unit. I'd be happy to go. Just tell me when. After climbing one of your sand dunes, I'm dying to see more of the desert, and I think until the internal changes are made to the unit there's not much I can do there. So, when do we go?'

Now?

Tonight?

That was his libido talking, and he knew it could no longer be considered in this situation. She'd made if perfectly clear there'd be no more 'complications', as she'd put it, and it was only right that he should honour her request.

And she was right about the dalliance. Was that the word she'd used? Whatever might have happened between them, it could have been no more than that. How could he, who'd already failed one woman, and her child, take on responsibility for another?

Although to have a child...

He spoke before melancholy swamped him.

'I understand Phil has the alterations in hand for the space where the unit will be. The hospital tradespeople are beginning work in a couple of days,' he replied, when he realised his silence had stretched for far too long. 'Do you feel you need to be there to supervise that part?'

She bit her lip—something he hadn't seen her do, and rather wished she wasn't doing so now given the way his intention strayed to the pinkness.

'I can't see that I'd be needed,' she said eventually. 'Would we have mobile coverage or access to telephones? Some way for Phil to reach me if he needed to ask me something?'

Phil again!

'In most areas,' Khalifa assured her. 'It might be called the Endless Desert but it's not the end of the world.'

She smiled at his defence of his country and he realised this trip might be a big mistake. Wasn't he supposed to be spending less time in this woman's company, not more? Hadn't he decided that only hours earlier?

Then Rimmi was speaking, asking how he'd travel, who he'd take with him, whether they would be staying overnight and what arrangements she should make for the doctor's comfort.

Mori was explaining Rimmi's words to Liz, who was looking more puzzled by the moment.

'When your grandmother wants to know how you'll travel, she's not talking camels, is she, because right now I'm not sure—'

He had to laugh.

'I think she meant helicopter or car,' he explained. 'Going by helicopter, we could cover a lot more villages and tribal camps in one day.'

Now Liz was frowning at him.

'But dropping out of the sky and telling these people stuff then whirling away again—isn't that what you're wanting to avoid? From what Mori tells me, most of the nomadic tribes now travel in four-wheel-drive vehicles and trucks, although they still keep camels. Aren't we better, if we're trying to introduce new ideas without changing their lifestyles too much, approaching them in a vehicle they're used to?'

It made sense, but before he could agree she was speaking again.

'And on that subject, I think if you're coming with me, you should come as a bloke, not a highness. Oh, they'll know who you are, but if you're in casual clothes—do you do casual clothes?—they might be more receptive. It seems to me the white gown puts up a kind of barrier, which you probably need at times, but in this case—'

She stopped suddenly, her fingers covering her mouth as if to stop more words coming out, her cheeks slightly flushed with embarrassment.

'I *do* talk too much!' she muttered from behind those long, slim fingers with their pale, unpainted nails.

'No, you're right,' he assured her. 'I see your point, but if we're to cover all the tribespeople we will, as my grandmother says, have to stay overnight, and though we'd be welcome in the camps you might enjoy the experience of a night in the desert. With inflatable mattresses and sleeping bags it can be quite comfortable. What do you think?'

And what was *he* thinking, even to be considering spending a night in the desert with this woman? He, who knew the magic the desert skies could weave, the mischief the djinns could get up to? He'd forget the night in the desert and work it so they stayed in a village—all villages had buildings in which to put up guests.

'I can manage an inflatable bed, although getting into a sleeping bag might be a bit tight,' Liz responded, then she smiled, and her eyes shone with excitement as she said, 'But, oh, a night in the desert! I've never dreamt I'd experience such a thing! It would be fantastic!'

So there he was, stuck. But if he took Saif to set up camp and cook—wouldn't that be best? Although taking Saif when they were visiting the tribespeople would be a bit like wearing his kandora and headscarf—proclaiming his leadership by bringing a retinue, if only a retinue of one.

Saif in another vehicle—would that be best?

'What are you thinking, my boy?' Rimmi asked, and he turned to her, wondering just what she meant by the question.

'Are you doubting the wisdom of my taking the woman into the desert to speak to the tribespeople?' he asked, and she smiled and shook her head.

'Not at all, the idea is a good one for, if you remember, it was mine. I am wondering about the thoughts that make you frown?'

Khalifa was sure his frown had deepened, for he could hardly tell his grandmother he feared taking the woman into the desert because he lusted after her. She would remind him Liz was a visitor and order him to put such thoughts from his mind.

At least, he thought she would, and now she was waiting for his answer.

'I wouldn't like Dr Jones to be uncomfortable,' he said.

Rimmi smiled.

'I think Dr Jones is more than capable of looking after

her own comfort,' she said. 'And I think it is you who will be uncomfortable, although you must be aware she will get tired. Make sure she rests in the afternoon and do not let her overstrain herself.'

Khalifa eyed his grandmother suspiciously. The older he got, the more he suspected the woman could read his mind, especially the bits of it he'd preferred remain unread.

Liz wondered what the pair was saying. Mori had stopped translating so obviously it was some private conversation, although Liz had heard Khalifa use her name.

The meal continued, more dishes appearing, more strange morsels of food to try, but finally Liz pushed aside her plate and turned to Mori.

'I realise it might be rude to leave the table, but I really need to stand up and walk around. Could you please explain that to Rimmi?'

Mori had barely nodded when Khalifa got to his feet, spoke to his grandmother, then reached out to support Liz as she struggled upright.

'Too much food,' she said, hoping to conceal the sizzling heat his touch was transferring to her hand.

She looked down, wishing there was some way she could offer Rimmi a direct apology, but when she tried, the old woman held up her hand and spoke through Mori.

'My grandson will take you for a walk in the garden. In your condition you must do this before you go to bed. It will help you sleep.'

Liz thanked her and followed Khalifa from the room, waving a general farewell to the women and children. A walk in the garden was just what she needed, but with Khalifa?

Perhaps if they talked about work...

She paused outside the door to push her feet into her

sandals, keeping her hand on the wall to balance herself so there was no need to touch Khalifa again.

'I know Dr Hassan had two special-care cribs flown down with her when she came. If we take one of them, would it leave the hospital short?' she asked, as they walked down the steps and onto the main path through the garden.

Khalifa didn't answer, although he paused and she stopped, just a little ahead of him, and looked back to where he stood, a dark figure lit by small lanterns burning at intervals along the path.

'Look around you. Do you really want to talk of work out here in the magic of the moonlight and the beauty of the garden?'

She smiled before she answered.

'Yes, I do,' she said firmly. 'Magic's all well and good, but it doesn't save babies, neither will it help the women of these desert tribes you talk of to visit a doctor or nurse if they need it during their pregnancy.'

'Then, yes, we can take a crib and whatever else you need,' he replied, sounding distinctly grumpy. 'Tomorrow I will take you to the hospital and you can organise whatever you want. There, are you satisfied? Can we now walk in the garden in silence, doing no more than enjoying the beauty of the evening? It is for your peace of mind, so you will sleep well, that my grandmother suggested the walk.'

Peace of mind! That's a joke. Peace of mind with him around?

Liz wanted to yell at him, to rail against the feelings he stirred in her without any apparent effort on his part. But it seemed he'd accepted her edict on the kiss, that it had just been a kiss and they shouldn't make too much of it, and had withdrawn behind the persona of the perfect host.

Perhaps that was all he'd ever been, his talk of attraction to her just that—talk!

So she walked with him in the garden and slowly the fizzing and sparks died down and the peace and beauty of the place entered her soul.

'It *is* beautiful,' she said, pausing by the fountain, trailing her hand in the shimmering water. 'I am glad we walked.'

Well, good for her!

Khalifa's mood was savage. Walking beside this woman in this place that was so special to him had been nothing less than torture. Walking beside her and not touching her, not feeling the softness of her skin or tasting the ripeness of her lips, captured in a kiss in the shadows of an olive tree. His body ached to feel her softness, his arms to hold her, but in his heart he knew he couldn't, and his head told him it was just as well she'd put a stop to further dalliance—because once he did touch her, he wasn't sure he'd ever be able to stop.

He held himself up to his full highness bearing, but the façade cracked and fell apart when she put out a hand, slightly damp from playing in the fountain, and grasped one of his, splashing water, klutz-style, all down his kandora.

'Thank you for the walk. There must be magic in this garden to have given me such ease,' she said, as cool as the hand that still held his. 'I hadn't realised just how badly my body needed to absorb some peace and beauty, to relax and let fate take its course. I've been pushing for things to fall into place, desperate for some certainty ahead, but now I realise I need to be patient and let whatever happens happen.'

He took her other hand and looked into her eyes, liking it that she was a tall woman, only a few inches shorter than his considerable height.

'You've had every reason to be lost in uncertainty,' he said, 'but I'm glad our garden brought you peace. Use it whenever you like, stay as long as you like. You will be looked after here and when, as you say, whatever happens happens, we will deal with that then.'

She smiled and he had to grip her hands more tightly because the urge to lean forward and take off her ghastly glasses and then press kisses all over her moonlit face was so strong that only by anchoring himself to her could he resist.

He walked her back to the guest house and saw her safely into Mori's care, then headed home, already on the phone making arrangements for their journey. Phil Cutler could make himself useful getting the things Liz would need ready for the trip, and Saif could pack the necessities for a night in the desert.

Yes, he was tempting fate by spending a night with her in the desert, whose magic was even stronger than the magic of the garden, but if the garden had given her peace, how much more at ease would she be after a night in the desert? And now he knew the torment she'd been suffering in recent months, how could he not offer her that one night?

CHAPTER EIGHT

IT TOOK a day to get organised but they left before dawn the following day, Liz assuring Khalifa that she loved early mornings, which wasn't entirely true but she had been sleeping so fitfully lately that getting out of bed had become a relief.

Now, driving through the desert, she was glad they'd left early. Already the dark shadows cast by the waves of dunes were lightening and the sands were changing colour, turning from black and grey to red and gold, so she felt she was in a world filling with colour.

'It's so beautiful,' she murmured, hardly daring to speak lest noise break the spell that beauty had bound around her.

'And treacherous, never forget that,' Khalifa told her. 'The beauty can lull the unwary into thinking nothing bad can ever happen here, but the desert is a cruel master and must always be treated with respect.'

She turned away from the magic beyond the window to look at him.

'You sound as if you know that from experience—but surely you grew up in the city.'

He nodded, and although he was in casual clothes—jeans, even, and a polo shirt—she could see the strength of his breeding in his face and in the hands that held the wheel of the big vehicle with the same ease as a good horseman might hold the bridle of a mettlesome stallion.

'I was, but my father felt all his boys should know their heritage, so for two years, from ten to twelve, we lived with relatives down here in the Endless Desert. We dressed like them, hunted with them, rode on mock attacks on other tribes. We mended our camel saddles and horse's bridles, and learned to shoot while mounted. And, most fun of all, we began to train our falcons, the ones our father gifted us.'

She thought of boys she knew, sons of friends and colleagues, who were ten, and wondered.

'Did you enjoy it?' she had to ask.

He didn't answer immediately, looking out across the waves of dunes —a dry red ocean.

'In the end, I enjoyed it so much that I stayed another year. I still return to that tribe for time out whenever I can manage it. Others hated it, and seeing their discomfort I believed my father had been wrong to make it a blanket rule. My oldest brother, for instance, had his spirit broken here. He became a man who needed others to help him make decisions. Oh, he chose well with his advisors, and has been a great ruler for our country, but his heart was never in it. He felt rejected by the desert, so he rejected it.'

'Which is why you're so determined to do more for the people of the south,' Liz said, and he glanced her way and smiled.

'I'd never put that into words before, but now I have, I realise the truth of it. Yes, it *is* why I am so anxious to help the desert people, but to help them without pushing them into a life they may not wish to live.'

Liz wanted to ask more about his childhood experiences but she sensed he'd said all he wanted to say about it—possibly more than he'd wanted to say. So she sat and thought about it—about a small boy sent to live with strangers.

'I guess it's not that much different to sending kids to boarding school,' she decided, then realised she'd spoken out loud right when she'd decided not to talk more about it.

But Khalifa turned to her and grinned.

'Very much so,' he said, 'although totally different from the boarding school I eventually attended. But the family sends the child away to learn the ways of the tribe—even in Western civilisation this is the case.'

'I hadn't thought of it that way,' Liz admitted. 'I was just lucky we lived in a city with schools all around so boarding school wasn't necessary. Where did you go? And did you enjoy it?'

'England, and no,' he said. 'It was cold and wet and always grey—can you imagine that after living with this colour? But the people were kind, and I learned things I couldn't have learned in the desert, things I needed to know to help my country move forward. I suppose you could say I learned the ways of other tribes.'

'And things you needed to know if you wanted to practise medicine,' Liz suggested, and again he grinned.

'Of course. Actually, I soon realised I wasn't very diplomatic, so decided my way to help my country would be through service of another kind. Medicine appealed to me.'

'Yet now you must be diplomatic,' Liz pointed out, wanting him to smile again.

But he shook his head.

'Not very. But, like my brother, I have people around me who can do the diplomatic niceties. The one good thing about the highness business is that people don't expect too much of you. A bow of my head, a touch of my hand, perhaps a smile from time to time, that's really all that's required of me in public.'

Not only was he not smiling but his voice had deepened, darkened at the edges by something like despair.

Why?

'Do you hate it so much?' Liz asked the question quietly, disturbed by the tension that seemed to have built up in the car.

He shook his head then glanced her way again.

'I do not hate the job,' he said, 'but what it did to me.'

Now he'd really stopped talking, Liz decided, and although she longed to know what he had meant, she stayed silent, looking out at the now fully lit landscape, marvelling at the colours all around her.

And there, ahead, in the gold and red and orange of the desert, she spied a darker shadow. As they drew nearer, the darkness turned to green, the huge fronds of the date palms shining in the sunlight.

'An oasis?'

'Our first stopping place,' Khalifa told her. 'This is a small village, too small to have a clinic, but the old midwife here has been handling minor accidents and illnesses for nearly fifty years. She is the power in the village, for all there is a chief who thinks he is.'

Liz smiled, thinking of the many women she knew who were the powers behind various thrones, from the personal assistants of big businessmen to the wives of politicians.

Although...

'If she's been running things her way for fifty years, will she be willing to listen to what I have to say?'

Khalifa turned towards her, and now he smiled, something she wished he wouldn't do, as her body was already excited about being in the car with him and her toes could only take so much curling.

'She has already visited the hospital to see what we have there and has probably set herself up with enough medicines to cure the entire population of the Endless Desert so, yes, she will listen. Not only will she listen but she will be happy to pass on what she learns to others.'

Looking around, Liz had to wonder if it was the desert that made the little oasis seem so isolated. They'd driven less than three hours from Najme, yet as the cluster of mud brick houses became obvious, it seemed to Liz that they were in the middle of nowhere.

'Ha! News of our visit has spread!' Khalifa said, pointing to a row of dust-covered vehicles drawn up at the edge of the village. 'Those belong to one of the remaining nomad tribes. They must be camped somewhere nearby at the moment.'

'And they've come to listen to me talk about preemie babies?' Liz queried, as Khalifa stopped the car and she saw that most of the visitors were men. 'It seems highly unlikely.'

Khalifa smiled again.

'It *is* highly unlikely. It's far more probable that they're here to ask a favour of me, or to tell me how badly a neighbouring tribe is behaving, or to offer me a daughter or sister as a new wife.'

His smile widened.

'Perhaps having a very pregnant companion will be a good thing after all.'

'I don't know about the "after all" part of that sentence,' Liz told him, 'but feel free to use my presence as a marriage deterrent, should you feel you need it.'

It had been a light-hearted moment, so she was surprised when he touched her fleetingly on the arm and said, 'Would that I could.'

His comment, as far as Liz was concerned, made no sense at all, but as a very elderly woman had emerged from one of the houses and was waving and smiling brightly at the new arrivals, Liz set the puzzle aside and concentrated on her job.

Khalifa greeted the woman with a kiss on both cheeks then, to Liz's surprise, he lifted the woman in the air and swung her around as he had with the children at the guest house.

She flapped and slapped at his arms but the smile on her face told Liz he was a welcome and much-loved visitor.

'This is Jazillah,' he said to Liz. 'Jazillah, this is Dr Elizabeth Jones.'

'Just call me Liz,' Liz responded, then turned to Khalifa as she realised they were both speaking English.

'I learned English from a friend,' Jazillah explained, taking Liz's hand in hers and turning it over as if to examine the lines on it.

The older woman held it, studying it, while Liz took in the dark colouring henna had left on Jazillah's hand.

'You are well, but troubled,' Jazillah finally declared, giving Liz back her hand. 'I know your machines can tell if there is cancer in someone's bones but are there machines yet that can probe the problems of the heart and mind?'

'Not yet, and probably not ever,' Liz told her, while Khalifa lifted the crib and other equipment they'd brought with them out of the back of the vehicle.

He carried it to the front porch of the house from which Jazillah had appeared, and set it down, and to Liz's surprise other women emerged from the tiny dwelling—surely too many to have been waiting inside.

Some, she saw, were pregnant, while others were probably grandmothers by now. A few were young, teenagers maybe, all cloaked in black, their hair covered, although their faces were visible.

'Serves me right for being suspicious,' Khalifa whispered from behind her. 'The men have not come begging favours but have brought their women in. That is good.'

Then, in a louder voice, he greeted the women in their own language, before telling Liz that Jazillah would translate and he would spend some time with the men.

As he departed, Liz watched the women folding themselves neatly and effortlessly down to sit on the ground. They were all attractive women, some of the young ones beautiful with huge doe-like eyes and clear olive skin.

Prospective brides for the ruler?

Liz smiled to herself and let the women settle, then introduced herself and explained what she did, thankful she had the excuse of showing the crib to avoid having to sit on the ground.

Though the sitting was relatively easy compared to the getting up.

'Sometimes babies are born too early, or are born with problems that mean they need special care in order to survive. I am the kind of doctor who can give them that care. I look after new babies, especially ones with problems.'

She paused while Jazillah translated and the women chattered among themselves, Jazillah explaining that they were talking of babies they knew who had died and remembering things that had gone wrong.

'Some of the things that can go wrong can be picked up during pregnancy through a scan,' Liz continued. 'Khalifa tells me that there are facilities for pregnant women to have a scan at the clinics in the larger villages. Sometimes it is possible to make things right for the baby even before it is born.'

She paused again, and again listened to the chatter.

As the group quietened, she showed them the crib and explained how everything attached to it worked, adding,

'For a baby born too early, we try to give it everything it would have received if it had still been in the womb.'

Now the questions began, and as she answered them, always with the lag for the translation, she began to wonder just how many villages they would manage to visit, and to wish someone had produced a chair, and to hope that soon they'd have a break so she could make a bathroom visit.

She was rescued by Jazillah, who apparently had the gift of reading minds as well as palms.

'We will break for coffee and you will drink mint tea,' the older woman decreed. 'But first you might like the bathroom. Come!'

She led Liz through the tiny house to the back, where a sparkling new bathroom had been added.

'It is good Khalifa spent time in the desert as a child, for he understands our needs,' Jazillah told Liz, then she slipped away.

By the time Liz returned, a chair had materialised beside the crib, and a small table beside it held a cup of mint tea and a selection of biscuits and fruit.

The women continued to talk while they sipped coffee from their tiny cups and ate dates and biscuits, so every now and then Jazillah turned to Liz to translate a question. Eventually they got on to the hospital, and all the services offered there, including the setting-up of the new unit.

'Will we be able to stay with our baby?' was the first question, and Liz assured the women they would be welcome there, then went on to explain about the verandas where family could also come and go so the woman had the support she needed.

'And men, they can visit?' Jazillah asked, and when she translated Liz's reply that the father could spend time in the unit with the baby, it raised a great deal of merriment among the women.

'They are telling me which of their husbands might do such a thing and which of them would be too scared of showing their emotion if their baby needed help,' Jazillah said.

Liz had to laugh.

'It's the same everywhere. It hurts fathers to see their baby in trouble, but often they don't want others to see their tears.'

More chatter and more questions, then finally Liz felt she'd covered as much as she could. She also had the sense that the women were accepting of the things she had told them and would be less reluctant to use the services Khalifa was providing.

But she was exhausted.

Had the language barrier made a fairly simple task more difficult, or were the effects of a busy first week in this strange land finally making themselves felt?

'You must rest now,' Jazillah decreed, perhaps not reading Liz's mind but seeing fatigue in her bearing.

'But we have other villages to visit, other people to see,' Liz protested.

'After you have rested.' Jazillah was firm. 'I have prepared a bed for you. Come!'

And suddenly Liz was happy to be led, to be bossed around and told to rest. In fact, she felt almost weepy that someone was taking care of her, as if her mother had returned from the dead and taken over just when she was needed.

Jazillah showed her a thick mattress on a floor just inside the door. It was covered by a bright, woven cloth and looked so inviting Liz forgot about the problems of getting up again from ground level, and sank down on it, turning on her side to get comfortable and falling asleep almost immediately.

Khalifa realised she was missing when he saw the empty chair, but the other women were still chatting on the porch so he assumed Liz had taken a short break. Jazillah soon put him right.

'You are not looking after that woman.' Her reprimand was sternly delivered, her face serious. 'You must make her rest and treat her well or her baby will be needing one of those special cribs you are carrying around.'

'Where is she?' he demanded, seriously disturbed by Jazillah's words.

'She is resting and she will stay resting until I say she can continue in the car,' Jazillah told her. 'And don't tell me you have to do a doctor check of her. I have checked and all is well, but she is very tired. And she is unhappy. Is that your doing?'

Here I am, leader of the country—and I'm being told off by an ancient medicine woman! Khalifa thought, but he was troubled by Jazillah's reading of the situation.

'She has reason to be unhappy,' he said quietly, 'and, no, not because of me.'

Unfortunately, his head added, although he knew full well he'd never willingly do anything to make Liz unhappy.

'Then you must take extra care of her,' Jazillah decreed. 'Unhappiness is bad for the baby, and is just as likely to cause problems as a medical condition.'

He frowned at that. Did she mean it? Had she proof?

Uncertain what to do next, he packed the crib and other paraphernalia back into the car. Though he longed to enter the house, if only to look at Liz, he remained outside, walking instead to the oasis, speaking to men who were there, fixing one of old pumps that fed water into the irrigation channels that ran between the date palms.

They talked of the prospects of the season's crop of

dates, of the likelihood of sandstorms over summer, and of village politics. A new headman was making his mark, but not everyone liked him—would Khalifa keep an eye out for trouble?

The typical village talk soothed him, although the little niggle of anxiety he felt over Liz's health refused to go away.

'Exhausted? What nonsense,' she told him only minutes later when he returned to the house to find her not only rested but ready to move on again. 'All I needed was a nap. I don't sleep well at night, but a nap now and then makes up for it. Where next?'

The blue eyes challenged him to argue and he glanced towards Jazillah and shrugged.

'Just make her rest,' the older woman said, then, to Khalifa's surprise, she took both of Liz's hands in hers and said, 'I will see you again soon. Soon and often.'

'I hope that doesn't mean I'm about to go into labour and you'll have to rush me back here for her to deliver the baby,' Liz joked as they drove away from the village.

'Don't joke about it,' Khalifa told her, more disturbed than Liz would realise by Jazillah's pronouncement. 'And, unlikely as it might seem to that woman, I *am* a doctor and I *can* deliver babies!'

'I'm sure you can,' Liz responded soothingly, 'but let's hope it doesn't come to that.'

He hoped it wouldn't as well, but there was no denying that his conversation with Jazillah had unsettled him and he was more than half-inclined to turn the vehicle around and head back to Najme.

'Don't even think about it.'

Liz's words made him realise he'd actually taken his foot off the accelerator as he considered this move.

'Are you reading my mind?' he demanded.

'Only the obvious bits,' Liz told him, then she reached out and touched his forearm. 'I'm not stupid, Khalifa. I know I have to look after myself. Yes, I was more tired than I realised this morning, but I'll take that as a warning and rest whenever I can. Let's do the next place then see how I feel, okay?'

Her touch had burned his skin—burned it as surely as a brand would have. How could that happen? How could it be that a foreign, pregnant woman could have sneaked beneath his emotional guard and be firing his body with need and his mind with any number of erotic fantasies?

And worse, he had yet to spend the promised night in the desert with her! In the desert where he was most alive, beneath the stars he knew like the skin on his own body, and with djinns around making mischief and no sand sprite to undo their spells…

Liz was glad the conversation about her health seemed to have finished, and was equally pleased to be travelling in silence. It meant she would think. And she needed to think. She needed to work out if her fatigue was simply physical or if the added complication of her attraction to Khalifa was contributing to it. Certainly, it took a lot of effort to pretend the attraction didn't exist.

'Oh!' she said, as they topped a dune and the wonder of the sight before her eyes drew the breathless exclamation.

Khalifa stopped the car so she could take in the great lake spreading from the bottom of the dunes.

'I can't believe it,' she finally said.

He smiled and said, 'Nor should you. It is a mirage.'

'No, it can't be, it's too real!'

'Unfortunately it is. It's often here and there are various explanations for it. Some say it's a reflection of the water in the oasis bounced back somehow from the sky but the oasis is surrounded by palms and very little of the water is visible so it seems unlikely. Science tells us it's caused by the deflection of light rays but to me it always has a kind of magic about it, and a lesson for us poor humans as well.'

'That things aren't always what they seem?' Liz guessed, and he nodded, then smiled and touched her baby bump.

'You'd be a prime example of that,' he said quietly, then he put the car into gear and drove down the dune, while Liz watched the water disappear and sand take its place once again.

They drove on in silence, Liz relaxed enough to find herself nodding off, so she let the back of the seat down and slept properly for a while, waking only when Khalifa stopped the car.

'This is the village closest to where I lived when I was in the desert,' he explained as she sat up and looked around. 'It has a clinic, and the clinic sister will have rounded up all the women from far and near to come and listen to you. She will also do the translating.'

Liz left her study of the village to turn towards him.

'If there is a woman in every village who can translate, why did you need to come?'

Khalifa looked at her and smiled.

'This may sound very pompous to you, but my presence means they will take you and what you tell them more seriously. And while you are talking to the women, I am not discussing camel prices with the men but explaining all the same things to them. It is important to them that they know what the women know, for how else can they make decisions together with their families?'

Liz nodded.

'Now, the clinic sister here is English. She came to teach first then trained as a nurse in Al Jabaya when she saw the need for nurses in the Endless Desert. She is married to the headman of the village and they have four children.'

'Then she probably knows far more about what I'm going to talk about than I do,' Liz told him.

'Possibly,' he conceded, 'but we add gravity to things she tells the women. The visit is not wasted for that reason.'

Liz found herself shaking her head again—there was so much to learn about this country and its culture, a lifetime wouldn't suffice.

Not that she'd have a lifetime here, a voice in her head reminded her, making her feel a little sad and sorry for herself. Although when a woman, all in black but with greying blonde hair peeking from beneath her head-covering came bounding out of a house to greet them, she forgot about everything but the job she'd come to do.

'Good heavens, you're pregnant. What on earth is Khalifa thinking to be dragging you around the desert in your condition?'

'I wanted to come,' Liz assured her. 'After all, what's the use of having a special-care unit at the new hospital if no one wants to use it? I'm Liz, by the way.'

'Jane,' the other woman said, holding out her hand and shaking Liz's before turning to Khalifa to berate him in person.

'Just make sure she rests after lunch,' was all he said, as he dumped the crib and the other gear at the front door, then he kissed Jane's cheek and departed, heading for wherever the men must have gathered.

Jane led Liz inside the house.

'The women are in here,' she said, and as Liz's eyes adjusted to the gloom she saw a couple of dozen women crammed into the room, all of them already settled on the floor, the coffee pot in the centre of the room burbling on a tiny, portable, gas ring.

The session went well, aided, no doubt, by Jane's understanding of everything Liz was saying. It ended with a lunch of salad and fruit. Then, as Jane showed Liz into a room where she could rest, she dropped the bombshell that put all thought of sleep from Liz's head.

'I'm surprised that Khalifa's letting you do this, given how he hid his first wife away throughout her pregnancy.'

By the time Liz had caught the subtext of the words, Jane was gone and she couldn't protest that she wasn't Khalifa's wife and neither was it his baby she carried.

How could Jane have got that idea?

And, worse, who else might think it?

It was only as she was drifting off to sleep that she remembered Khalifa's words in the car when they'd been setting off—something about her pregnancy protecting him from men offering their sisters or daughters as brides?

Had he guessed people might assume the baby was his?

Was he using her?

CHAPTER NINE

REFRESHED from her sleep, Liz was able to take more notice of the landscape as they drove deeper into the desert. She'd set aside her silly suspicions about this journey with Khalifa, putting them down to tiredness and the added problems the attraction caused her body.

Now, looking around, she realised the scenery was changing.

'It's still sand and dunes, but it's different somehow,' she said, when she'd tried and failed to pin down the difference.

His smile lit up his face.

'I call this the real desert,' he said. 'It's rare a stranger notices it because the differences are subtle. The dunes are slightly higher, the red of the sand is deeper in colour, and the wind carves shapes along the top of the hills so now you see a dog, and in a minute it might be a crocodile.'

'You're right. Look there—a prancing horse!' Liz didn't try to hide her delight, and she watched, bemused, as the shape of the horse turned into a big swirl of a wave.

'Is the sand shifting so that the shapes change?' she asked, twisting in her seat to see what had happened to the wave.

'No, it's partly because we're moving, and partly because the sand is so pure down here—so uncontaminated by pollution of any kind—it reflects light in strange ways, giving the impression of shapes.'

'A different kind of mirage,' Liz whispered, looking all around her, trying to find other shifting shapes. 'No wonder the people believe in djinns and sand sprites when they see these transformations every day. How else would they explain them?'

Khalifa heard the wonder in her voice, and his heart hurt, for he'd never known a stranger even to see the shapes, let alone understand how his people felt about them. He wanted to stop the car and sit and hold her while they watched the dune shapes change in the shifting sunlight.

He wanted to stop the car and hold her.

He wanted to hold her.

That was the sum of it.

And this time it wasn't just his attraction to her prompting his thinking. It was something different, something deeper, something he didn't understand.

He didn't stop the car, driving on, driving just a little faster, hoping that once he was out of the car the feeling wouldn't be as strong.

'Damn it all, they must have moved on.'

Had she heard the frustration in his voice that she turned from her study of the landscape to look at him?

'Problems?'

None that he could tell her about!

'Not really,' he replied. 'I understood the next group was camped down there.' He pointed to where he'd expected them to be. 'Can you see the well?'

To his surprise Liz laughed.

'I'd like to say yes, but what I'm looking at will probably turn into an animal of some kind, then back into a

sand dune. You have wells? Out here in the middle of the
desert, there's water?'

The laugh had made his heart hurt even more, but he
covered his confusion with practicality.

'There's water everywhere under the desert. At the
oases it has come to the top, but out here we dig wells. In
fact, most of the wells are centuries old, dug by the nomadic tribes so long ago that no one remembers when.
The nomads are happier camping near wells, because at
most of the oases there are villages, and to the nomads
villages represent civilisation.'

She was frowning now, and that hurt him too, although
he knew it was just puzzlement on her part.

Or he hoped it was.

'But are there many nomadic people still living in the
desert?' she asked.

'Not as many as when I was a boy, but still up to ten
roaming tribes.'

She nodded and he knew she considered everything
he said and that her interest wasn't superficial. It was em-
pathy.

'Oh, now I see the well,' she cried, then turned back
to him. 'But what do we do next, now we know they're
not there?'

He drew up beside the well and *now* he stopped the car,
but not to hold her. Instead he stepped out and dropped
the bucket that stood on the rim, hearing it splash into the
water. He wound up a pail full of the fresh, clean liquid,
filled a beaker that was hung on the frame, filled it and
carried it around to where she'd just alighted from the car.

'Try it,' he said, then watched with pleasure as she
drank, tentatively at first then deeply, sighing with satisfaction at the end.

'Beautiful,' she said.

'But not as beautiful as you,' he murmured, taking the beaker and draining the last drops, then, with his lips still wet, he kissed her.

Liz was sure she didn't mean to kiss him back. She'd decided very firmly that kissing was off limits where this man was concerned. Probably, in her condition, where any man was concerned! But she was definitely kissing him back, leaning into him, tasting the water on his lips, tasting him, wanting more while her head rambled on about not kissing men.

Now her breasts were aching from the kiss, and she had to move so they could push against him, seeking relief, although his body heat made them ache even more, ache for his touch, for some release from the tension a simple kiss was causing in her body.

Except there was nothing simple about this kiss. If anything, it was the most complex kiss Liz had ever experienced, for it seemed to be saying things as well as asking things and she didn't understand any of it, except the need to keep on kissing Khalifa whoever, His Highness of Al Tinine...

The revving of an engine shattered the moment.

A vehicle approaching?

Out here in the desert?

She broke away from Khalifa, or maybe he broke away from her, although his hand stayed on her back, steadying her as yet another large, dusty vehicle approached them, driving not on the half-made road they'd been following, but rolling down a sand dune.

'Saif!' Khalifa muttered, dropping his hand from Liz's back and leaving a patch of skin that felt suddenly cold.

He walked away from her to meet the approaching vehicle, while Liz dipped the beaker into the bucket of water and sipped the clear, pure liquid once again, trying not to think of the kiss, and definitely not think of the reactions it had produced in her body. She focussed on the now—on what was happening—on why Saif had suddenly materialised, here in the middle of the desert.

She watched the two men talking, the low murmur of voices easily carrying across the silence of the desert, not that she could understand a word that was being said.

Khalifa's head was bent towards Saif, and Liz could study him, trying to make out why this man, of all the men she'd met at different times in her life, should affect her the way he did.

It wasn't that he had power—she'd barely been aware of that before they'd arrived in his country. And she knew plenty of men with money, so it wasn't the jet or the palace. It was just something about the man—something more than physical attraction, she was sure of it.

He was walking back towards her. Saif was already back in his vehicle, preparing to drive off.

'Is there a problem?' Liz asked Khalifa as he approached, while just looking at him walk towards her made her heart beat faster.

The smile he offered by way of answer sent her pulse into a further frenzy and she reached out to hold the top of the well in case her knees became too unreliable to hold her up.

'No problem, but Saif assumed we'd come here in search of the nomads. He tells me they're camped at the next well. It's some distance away, so we'll go to the camp he's set up for us and visit them in the morning.'

Liz studied him for a moment, trying hard to read his face but finding no clue about his feelings in it.

'Are you suggesting we stop now because you're worried I'll get overtired?' she asked, and the smile returned.

'I'd like to use that as an excuse, but I'm suggesting

we stop for my own selfish reasons. Saif brought out my
favourite bird and I'd like her to fly before dusk. She can
catch her dinner, if she's not too out of practice.'

'Your bird? A falcon?'

Liz breathed the words, unable to believe she was going
to see a hunting bird in flight—unable to believe an already amazing day could get even more extraordinary.

'Let's go,' Khalifa said, and he took her arm and led
her to the car, opening the door for her then helping her
in, something he'd done before, but this time it seemed...

More intimate?

No, she was imagining it—building on the kiss and the
impact it had had on her body.

He was in the car himself now, starting the engine, his
long, slim fingers relaxed on the steering-wheel.

Long slim fingers that had stroked her back—

Forget the kiss! Think of something else!

'You said Saif had set up our camp. You sent him out
to do this?'

Khalifa glanced her way and smiled again.

'I didn't send him,' he said, a little stiff now. 'I am more
than capable of setting up a camp but he insisted on doing
it, or maybe Rimmi gave him his orders. All he'd say was
that he wanted us to be comfortable, and to be sure there
was food you could eat. He doesn't trust me as a cook.
The bird was a surprise, something I hadn't expected.'

'But he knew it would please you? He knows you so
well?'

He didn't turn this time, all his concentration on getting the vehicle up the sand dune, but he nodded, then
said, 'Probably too well,' in such a rueful voice Liz had
to wonder what he'd meant.

It seemed they must have driven up and over and down
at least forty more dunes before once again she saw, in

the distance, a dark shadow on the ground. As they drew nearer it materialised into a tent, but a tent unlike any Liz had ever seen. It was broad and low-set, slung a mere five feet above the ground, the sides sloping down onto the sand, poles and ropes holding and anchoring it.

'In the past, the tents were made from camel skins, the rugs woven from either camel or goat hair. These days the tents are made from factory-made fabric, but still keep the dark colouring of the originals, and the rug-weaving is still practised.'

He pulled the car up to one side of the tent and Liz saw, set out in front of it a brightly patterned rug and a stack of firewood, while a small fire was set beyond the rug. She could picture the scene from times gone by, with the men, backs to the tent, looking out past the fire into the darkness, looking out for trouble! Inside the tent she could make out two flat mattresses, not unlike the ones she'd been resting on earlier in the day. There was also a low table and, incongruously, a number of cool boxes, no doubt containing the dinner Saif didn't trust Khalifa to cook.

She slipped out of the car and stretched, then looked around for her companion, finding him bent over a box in the shade of the tent. Moving closer, she could tell it was the kind of cage used to carry small cats or dogs, and as Khalifa slipped a heavy gauntlet onto his arm, she realised the bird he'd spoken of, his falcon, was in the cage.

'May I come closer?' she asked, uncertain just how falcons might take to strangers.

'Of course,' Khalifa told her. 'She's wearing her hood so you won't frighten her.'

'More likely she'll frighten me,' Liz joked, but Khalifa was concentrating on the cage, undoing the latches then putting his gauntleted hand close to the ground, murmuring to his bird, words Liz couldn't understand.

The bird hopped out. She was far smaller than Liz had imagined, perhaps the size of an owl. She saw what Khalifa had meant by the hood, a little leather cap on the bird's head. It was sitting on the glove now, and she could see strings coming from around its legs, the strings now clasped between Khalifa's fingers.

'She's beautiful,' Liz whispered, taking in the snowy breast of the bird and the dark bands of colour on her back and wing feathers. Khalifa was petting her, stroking her, talking soothingly, and it seemed to Liz the bird understood exactly what he was saying. He took the hood off her head and she turned to look at him, her eyes bright and inquisitive.

'She looks like you,' Liz told him, as she saw the two heads in profile, both imperious, haughty, aware of their power and the attraction of it.

Khalifa raised his eyebrows then spoke again to the bird, carrying her away from the tent, holding his arm up, then releasing the strings he'd held between his fingers.

Wide wings raised high, the bird seemed to stretch, then she lifted into the air, circling as she rose with what seemed like effortless ease until she grew so small it was hard to see her. Just a speck, circling and circling.

'She must have fantastic eyesight if she can spot her prey from that height,' Liz said.

Just as she spoke the bird dived, arrowing towards the ground before rising again, a smaller bird in its talons.

'Oh!'

'Do you find it cruel?' Khalifa asked, correctly interpreting Liz's exclamation.

'Not cruel, because she has to eat—we all do. But it was unexpected, I suppose. I had no idea what she'd eat.'

'Quail tonight—but in the past the birds hunted to feed the families who bred and kept them. There's very little

food in the desert and often whatever the birds caught
was the only protein the families ate. Now it is sport, but
back at Najme for sport we use small stuffed bunnies and
birds that are flung from a bow to give the bird the impression of movement.'

The bird had returned, dropping the quail at Khalifa's
feet and returning to perch on his gauntlet.

'I'll feed her now and then she will fly without hunting, fly just for the delight of it, to feel the air beneath her
wings and the air currents carrying her upwards.'

He took the two birds back towards the shade, and Liz
sensed he regretted letting her see the kill, as if it—or her
reaction to it—had changed something between them.

She followed him and watched, understanding that she
couldn't judge either bird or man. The bird had followed
its nature, it had been born knowing it had to hunt to eat.

'I do understand,' she said, squatting awkwardly beside
him, wanting more than anything to recapture the closeness they'd shared at the well.

Wanting him to kiss her again? her head asked.

Probably, was the honest answer.

Her meal finished, the falcon hopped back on Khalifa's
arm and he held it high until the bird took off again.

'Do you want to catch her?' he asked, pulling off the
gauntlet and offering it to Liz.

'Would she come to me?'

He dug in his pocket and produced a whistle.

'Put on the glove then blow this and hold your hand
up high.'

Excitement rose as Liz pulled on the heavy leather covering, then put the tiny whistle to her lips. It made a sharp,
high-pitched sound, barely heard, yet the bird turned in
the air and as Liz raised her arm, it dived straight down,

alighting, not at three hundred and fifty kilometres an
hour but as lightly as a feather on the glove.

'Oh!' she whispered, this time in utter wonder, for the
bird, close up now, was even more beautiful than she'd first
thought, the soft feathers gleaming in the last rays of the
sun, the proud head turning this way and that.

Khalifa guided Liz's hand down towards a stand. The
bird stepped onto it and looked around, her bright eyes
taking in her surroundings.

'Will she stay there?' Liz asked.

'I'll attach a leash to her jesses, the little strings that
hang down from her anklets, and fix her there so she's
safe. But I don't think she'd fly away unless she was startled by something.'

'She's amazing,' Liz said, spellbound by the beauty
of the bird.

'She is,' Khalifa said, and he put his arm around Liz
as she stood looking, and the arm made her wonder if he
was still talking about the bird.

He guided her towards the tent.

'Will you relax inside, or should I bring some pillows
out to the rug beside the fire?'

It was such an ordinary question Liz forgot about there
being subtext in his conversations. He was nothing more
than a kind man, and his touch was simply supportive,
while the kiss…

Well, the kiss could have been nothing more than happiness at being back in his special place in the desert and
wanting to share his delight.

'Outside, please,' she replied. 'I could sit and watch the
desert change for ever.'

He turned towards her as if to say something, then
shook his head and ducked into the low tent, returning

with one of the padded mattresses and a couple of big cushions in his arms.

'Sit!' he ordered when he'd arranged them to his satisfaction on the rug.

He held her arm, supporting her weight, while she sank down onto the ground, then he insisted she make herself comfortable, helping adjust the cushions behind her back.

'A drink? I'll check what Saif has left us, but there is sure to be some iced tea, and I would think pomegranate juice if you'd like something more exciting.'

Liz smiled up at him.

'I think pomegranate juice is appropriate for the desert,' she said, stretching back against the cushions and smiling to herself as he disappeared into the tent.

'You are happy?' he asked when he returned.

She had to pause and think about it, then answered honestly.

'I am,' she said. 'Right now, this very minute, all my problems seem so far away, and being pampered, offered drinks, being waited on—that's special.'

He squatted beside her to hand her the drink, his dark gaze scanning her face.

'I imagine you are far too independent to accept much pampering,' he said, easing into a sitting position beside her—close but not too close.

She was about to agree, then remembered.

'Actually,' she admitted, 'I was showered with pampering when I first became pregnant. Bill and Oliver couldn't do enough for me. It was all I could do to take off my own shoes when I stayed overnight for a visit.'

Khalifa took her free hand and squeezed her fingers, although this was the first time he'd heard her speak of her brother and his partner with sadness but not deep pain in her voice.

'Everything will be all right,' he told her, and although it was an empty promise when so much in her life was in limbo, she accepted it with a smile and lifted her glass towards him.

'Cheers!' she said.

'*Shucram*!' he replied, lifting an imaginary glass and touching it to hers.

'*Shucram*? Is it Arabic?'

'It is what we say as a toast. You like the word?'

'I do,' Liz agreed and raised her glass again. '*Shucram*!'

It was a nothing conversation, words passing back and forth, but something else was passing back and forth as well—awareness.

Or was it only one-way traffic, he wondered, this tingling in his skin, the rush along his nerves, the tightening of his body?

She was pregnant!

Yes, but try as he might to reject the thought, he was beginning to believe that he found her pregnancy just as sexy as the rest of her. At first he'd thought it was just the hair, and then the way she laughed, and her creamy skin, and her eyes behind the glasses. But the pregnancy definitely wasn't offputting, and the more he got to know the woman inside the outer shell, the more the attraction grew.

'Are you not having a drink?' she asked, and he heaved himself off the rug and headed for the tent, not for a drink but to collect his thoughts.

He fished around in the cool boxes and found that the ever-reliable Saif had packed snacks, even labelling the flat platters with a sticker—'Use these for snacks'. Saif really did think his boss was an idiot.

Idiotic right now.

He wasn't even sure if he was reading the signs of a

mutual attraction—kissing him back, pressing her body into his—correctly.

He put the snacks onto the platter, removing the sticker first, then poured himself a glass of juice and returned outside.

Liz was lying back, looking all around her, wide eyes taking in the beauty of the desert as the shadows grew longer and the sinking sun left the dunes black-shadowed and mysterious. But the sky was brightening in the west and soon the colours of the sunset would be reflected in the crystalline sand, so they'd be afloat in a sea of red and gold and orange, even vermillion and saffron, these last two better words because they held some of the beauty of the colours.

It held them silent, the nightly transformation of the desert sands, and only when the colours faded and dusk fell about them did Liz move, putting down her glass on the platter and turning to lie on her side, looking at Khalifa.

'I can see why you stayed an extra year,' she said quietly. 'As well as its spectacular beauty, this place brings a sense of peace, doesn't it?'

'It's because you can't fight it and win,' he told her. 'You can only survive in the desert if you learn to live with it, learning all its many moods, bending to its will rather than trying to bend it to yours. The road we followed to the oasis and the well is a great example. It was built by my brother to open up the desert, but slowly and surely the desert is reclaiming it. Not that it matters when we have vehicles that can traverse the sand, but no man can tame the desert.'

'Neither should they want to,' Liz said. 'We've already tamed too much of the world's land, and we need these wild places to—would it sound silly if I said to replenish our souls?'

He moved the tray so he could touch her face.

'Definitely not silly,' he said.

He wanted to touch more of her, to feel his hands slide over her skin, to lift her hair and kiss the nape of her neck beneath it, to lie with her so their bodies learned the shape and texture of each other.

'I'll get our dinner. Knowing Saif, he'll have stuck to cold meats and salads so I don't have to show my lack of cooking prowess, but as it's getting cool, I'll light the fire anyway.'

He edged away from the distraction of Liz and lit the fire, then went into the tent and lit the lantern and the candles Saif had left for them.

The light was soft, but it was enough for him to discover his guess had been right. Inside the largest of the cool boxes were platters of meat, already laid out, and salads in bowls. The last of the cool boxes held an array of fruit. That, he'd leave until later.

He brought out food, setting it beside his guest so she could reach everything with ease. Plates followed, and damp napkins in a thermos flask so they were still warm and faintly scented.

'A feast in the desert,' Liz murmured as she filled her plate with bits and pieces of salad and meat, trying everything as he'd been sure she would because this was a woman who lived for new experiences.

Yet she'd given up nine months of her life to produce a child for her brother? How much she must have loved him! How great her capacity for love!

'You're not eating,' she told him, pointing at him with her fork.

'Thinking,' he said, and she smiled.

'Thinking makes me hungry,' she said, then laughed at herself. 'Actually, everything makes me hungry these days. But I'd feel a lot better about stuffing myself with food if you were at least nibbling on a lettuce leaf.'

He filled his plate and ate, enjoying the food, enjoying the company, enjoying most of all the desert, his spiritual home.

Liz wondered what he was thinking. Probably not how sexy she was, although his sexiness was one of the main topics of thought running through *her* mind. Something about the man stirred bits of her that had never been stirred before and she wasn't entirely certain it was all physical attraction. The more she saw and learned of him as a man—the way the people obviously loved him, the way he never spoke down to anyone, his tenderness with his grandmother—the more attractive he became.

While she was the very opposite—fat and even clumsier than usual, her life in chaos—no redeeming features at all, so why he kept on kissing her she had no idea.

Kept on kissing her? It had happened, what, twice?

But even thinking of the kisses had her body stirring, her breasts growing heavy, her skin going coming out in goose-bumps.

She set down her plate, afraid she'd start trembling, and looked at the dancing flames of the fire in front of them.

Fire, heat, burning…her attraction to this man could lead nowhere, so why get burnt?

Because I want to?

She hadn't really expected an answer to her silent question, so when it came it shocked her. What was she saying? That she'd like to make love to this man for the sheer physical pleasure of it?

Knowing nothing would come of it?

Knowing it would probably be a one-off experience?

Knowing she'd have something to remember him by—

that was the real answer—a memory of a special night in a very special place with a very, very special man!

'*Are* you attracted to me?'

The question popped out without much forethought. Klutz!

She could feel the heat rising in her cheeks, burning there, but at least he was smiling.

'You have no idea how much,' he said softly, then he moved the platters and plates and shifted so he sat beside her, his body close but once again not touching her. 'But you are in a strange place, both physically and mentally. If we do something about this attraction, are you sure you won't regret it?'

She turned towards him and this time *she* touched *his* face.

'I won't regret it,' she said quietly, then she leaned forward and kissed him on the lips, tasting remnants of the pomegranate drink, tasting him.

The kiss was slow and easy, not tentative but definitely the beginning of a voyage of discovery. His tongue delved, invaded, starting the fires within, nothing more than glowing embers at the moment, but Liz knew they'd flare soon.

She slid her hand beneath his shirt to feel his skin, and heard his murmur—of pleasure? Of approval?—then felt his hand against her breast, felt her nipples growing hard, and raised her hand to touch his, to brush against them, gently, teasing the tight buds.

His murmur became a growl and now his lips had moved from hers, searching along her chin, finding skin to tease beneath her hair, shivers running down her spine. His tongue flicked against the hollow of her neck and this time it was she who murmured—cried out really—wanting more, so much more.

'I will take care of you.' He breathed the words against

her skin and before she could protest that their satisfaction should be mutual, his hand had sought the very centre of her being and with one hand on her breast and the other brushing gently but insistently against her panties, she found herself squirming with delight and need, squirming and breathing hard, wanting more yet wanting him to stop what was becoming torture.

But she, too, could tease, so she felt for him and found the hardness pressed against his jeans, finding the tip of it and running her fingers lightly over it.

'Clothes,' he gasped, and they separated, but though she longed to see him naked, she was less inclined to reveal her own body in all its swollen glory.

'I *have* seen pregnant women before,' he said gently, obviously reading her reluctance to disrobe.

And with that he lifted the loose top she wore up and over her head, then with seemingly practised ease he dispensed with her bra before reaching down and sliding off her long trousers and panties.

'You are beautiful,' he said, pushing away the arms she had wrapped around herself. 'Radiantly beautiful.'

'Fat,' she retorted, 'while you...'

He'd shucked off his own clothes and knelt beside her, the light from the flickering fire dancing on his naked skin.

She touched him, more in awe than anything, but he took her hand and kissed her palm, then drew her thumb into his mouth and suckled it, taunting her to distraction before turning his attention to her breasts, teasing at one with his tongue, at the other with what seemed to her like magic fingers.

The slow dance of foreplay began again. Liz finally relaxed, telling herself it was for the memory, and that she had to grab as much enjoyment as she could from it. But conscious thought soon disappeared, her body revelling in sensation, her brain numbed by delight. Unhurried by some unspoken but mutual consent, they explored each other's bodies, learning the shape of them, the taste and texture of the skin, the places where the slightest touch stirred the embers of desire, making them flicker until suddenly they became flames.

He lay behind her now, pleasuring her with his hands, building the tension in her body to gasping point then easing back until he was certain she was ready. Only then did he slide into her, gently and carefully, but still touching and teasing so she was lifted to another plane then burst apart, coming with a shuddering sob, then coming again as he, too, climaxed and held her tightly to him.

They lay together, the crackling of the dying fire the only noise in the empty desert, the stars above so bright Liz felt she could reach out and touch them, pull them down and hold them in her lap in the same way she held the happiness their lovemaking had given her.

'No regrets?' Khalifa whispered in her ear, and she snuggled closer to him.

'How could there be?' she queried softly. 'This is an experience that I'll treasure for a lifetime.'

His arms tightened around her, then one hand slid down to rest on her belly where the baby kicked obligingly.

Had it been mine, I would never have to let her go, her or her baby, Khalifa thought, then he wondered where the thought had come from. This woman could never be his, for all he was fairly certain he might love her.

Love her?

An even more bizarre thought to be having. What did he know of love?

Yet melancholy enfolded him as he held the woman in

his arms, and melancholy was something he never felt out here in the desert.

Did love always lead to sadness?

'Thank you,' the woman in his arms whispered softly, the words like a benediction.

He wanted to thank her, too, to talk about his feelings, but he didn't know how to start because men of his tribe didn't do that kind of thing.

'Talk to me,' she said—reading his mind.

She had turned so she faced him, resting her hand on his chest as if she needed to maintain physical contact with him.

'About what?' he countered, not certain enough of love to talk of it.

'About you,' she responded. 'About your wife—your feelings about the baby?'

She patted her naked belly and added, 'I've been so determined not to feel anything about this poor wee soul's arrival, I've no idea how a pregnant woman might feel, let alone a man. Were you pleased? Excited? Would you marry again? Have another child?'

Was there a shadow of pain behind her questions? Or was he imagining he heard it?

He didn't know, but she'd asked and now he wanted to answer her, to talk about Zara and his child as he had to no one else.

'My wife was over the moon, totally absorbed in her pregnancy, but me...?'

He hesitated.

'You will think this very silly, but to have a pregnant wife, somehow it is a confirmation of a man's virility. I was proud.'

Again he stopped, partly distracted by a finger drawing whorls around his nipple but also uncertain how to proceed.

'Keep talking,' the owner of the finger said, and now he found it easier.

'I was excited by the thought of a child, more than a baby. Seeing a child grow, explaining things as he or she explored and learned about the world.'

The finger stopped moving and in the moonlight he saw her turn her head so she could study him as she asked her next question—study him as he answered.

'And now?'

He touched the upturned face.

'Now I am a coward. Although I know if I had a pregnant wife I would be far more involved with her pregnancy, the guilt I felt—still feel—at not realising all was not going well for Zara would probably haunt me.'

She brushed her finger across his lips and asked, oh, so gently, 'Was there anything you could have done? Would being with her more have made a difference?'

He didn't want to answer, knowing answering would release him from his guilt, but his guilt was all he'd had of Zara after her death…

'Tell me.'

'No.'

The word came out far too bluntly. Could he really have *not* wanted to lose the guilt?

'I don't mean, no, I won't tell you but, no, there was nothing I could have done,' he said, more gently now, and going on to explain the genetic heart problem that had killed his wife and child, a problem that had never been known or even suspected.

The woman who'd prised this confession from him snuggled closer and reached out to clasp his head against her breast, running her fingers across his short hair, offering solace with touch.

He reached for her hands and held them, squeezing them gently, silently thanking her for the blessing of her understanding. Thanking her for pointing out how pointless his guilt had always been.

She eased her hands away and he touched the bulge of her pregnancy, running his hand over the taut skin, wishing...

Her hand closed over his.

'Thank you again,' she said, as if in telling her he'd given her some kind of gift, then she moved so she could lie in comfort, and whispered a quiet 'Goodnight'.

He lay, still propped on his elbow, watching how quickly she slid into sleep, feeling guilt—was he obsessed by it?—about their lovemaking, thinking she'd already been tired...

Once certain she was sleeping, he eased away from her and went into the tent to find a rug to cover her, but when he returned he simply stood and looked at her, bathed in starlight. He looked at the pale creamy skin, the spread of hair, the swollen belly that stirred him more than anything. To him, at this moment, she was the epitome of womanhood and he was pretty sure he loved her.

CHAPTER TEN

HE WAS asleep when Liz awoke to find herself covered by a soft, warm blanket. For a moment she lay there, remembering—first her body remembering, warming, delighting in reliving the sensations—then her mind remembered Khalifa's conversation and her heart ached for the pain he'd carried. Meanwhile, a tiny spark of delight glimmered in the darkness—delight that he'd talked to her about something so personal.

But remembering was wasting time, because right now she had pressing physical needs of a different kind. She eased herself away from him, trying not to wake him, then pulled on her clothes rather randomly, although it was stupid to think she had to get dressed when there was no one but the bird to see her as she crept around to the back of the tent for a bathroom break.

She squatted behind the tent, feeling the unfamiliar tenderness Khalifa's lovemaking had left behind, revelling in it and the sense of well-being in her body.

Satisfaction, that's what it was—satisfaction that had produced enormous pleasure and great release.

Straightening up, she looked up at the heavens, searching for the Southern Cross, although she knew she wouldn't see it in a northern sky. But all the stars looked friendly, and she thought about what people said—about stars aligning.

Her stars and Khalifa's had aligned, for just a short time, and now she had the memory of this very special night.

She sank her toes into the sand and wondered about the sand sprite. Had *her* lovemaking been as satisfying? Had it been so special that she'd had no regrets about having to remain a mortal?

'Sand sprites indeed!' Liz muttered, and she shook herself out of her fantasies and focussed on the purely practical.

Her teeth itched!

Could she risk opening the car to get out her small overnight bag?

She was walking towards it when she saw the bag sitting on the front of vehicle. She reached for it. She'd need to find water, maybe in the tent, so she could have a wash and clean her teeth.

And put on clean clothes.

She had opened the bag and was delving in it to find her toiletries when she felt the pain—a sharp jab, so agonising she forgot about the sleeping man and screamed, hopping around on one leg while she tried to find the source of the pain on her other ankle, hopping so she tripped and fell against the car, unable to stop her cry of dismay.

The scream came to Khalifa in a dream, but he was soon awake, aware Liz was no longer in his arms, aware it hadn't been a dream. He sat up, searching for her, angry he'd been so deeply asleep he couldn't place the direction the noise had come from.

'Liz?'

He heard his own panic in his cry, but her answer—

'I'm okay, something bit me and I fell'—did little to reassure him.

He rushed towards her voice, to find her struggling to
her feet beside the car.

'Stay still,' he ordered, and, with hands he knew were
shaking he bent to lift her, carrying her to the tent where
a lantern still glowed softly and placing her gently on the
couch.

'The bite, where is it?' he demanded, his voice so rough
she flinched, but she pointed to her leg and without hesita-
tion he stripped off her trousers, shaking them, seeing the
scorpion that fell from them, his heart stopping with fear
even as his foot lifted to squash the life out of it.

But squashed, would he be able to tell?

He brushed it further from her then lifted the lantern,
relief swamping him as he saw the square-shaped sternum
rather than the triangular shape of the deadly Leiurus.

Now he squashed it, then returned to Liz, kneeling beside her, examining the reddened mark on her calf.

'I'm sorry, I should have warned you about the little
beasts. It will be painful for a while, but it wasn't poison-
ous. Did you hurt yourself in the fall?'

Even as he asked the question his hands were moving
over her, calmer now, although not as calm as a professional's hands should be, for his heart was still racing, his
mind now caught up in the inevitable 'what ifs', his chest
tight with the knowledge that she could have died.

Had she felt his fear that she took his hands and looked
into his face?

'Khalifa, I'm fine. Yes, my leg hurts—it's like a bad
ant bite but that's all. Stop panicking.'

She smiled as she spoke, her beautiful, warm, open
smile, and although he'd have liked to tell her he never
panicked, the words wouldn't come because now he

couldn't breathe properly, he was so overwhelmed by the thought of losing her.

He wanted to tell her, to explain how he felt—how the revelation that had come to him when he'd looked at her body in the moonlight, and how hearing her cry had nearly killed him—but he'd lost her. Her eyes were no longer on him but looking inward. There was a small frown of concentration on her face.

'What is it?' he demanded, but she didn't reply, her hands moving to her belly, holding it.

Now new alarm spread through him, especially when he saw the movement—the bulge of her stomach tightening into a ball, obvious because she was so slim.

She was in labour?

Out here?

Now?

Great!

'Is it a contraction?' he demanded. 'Was that the first? Are you timing them? Are you in pain? Did you fall heavily?'

Or had their lovemaking brought it on?

Whatever the cause, it was he who had, selfishly, wilfully, wished to spend the night in the desert with her— he who had made love to her.

Now another woman and her baby's lives were in jeopardy.

'Khalifa.'

One word, just his name spoken softly, brought him out of his panic. He took her hands in his and looked into the blue eyes.

'I think this time it's for real,' she whispered, then stopped as another contraction ripped through her body, her hands clutching his, clamping on them, squeezing tightly.

'I'm sorry—such a nuisance,' she gasped as her grip loosened, telling him the pain was gone.

'Never!' he said. 'I might have put you in this position, Liz, with my own stupidity, bringing you out here, but I'll take care of you and the baby, believe me.'

She half smiled, although her abdomen was contracting again and the smile turned into a grimace, though she pushed out the words she wanted to say.

'Not your fault—no more guilt!' she told him, then grabbed his hands again as if they were her only lifeline, her main connection to reality.

And *he* should have been timing the contractions! They seemed to be coming far too close together, but she was right, no more guilt. This woman was *not* going to die! He was a doctor, he could deliver a baby, and even though it would be preemie, he could handle that until help arrived. Help would come. He had no radio contact here, but back at the well he could use his mobile and call in a helicopter to airlift Liz safely to the hospital.

She was resting, now, her face damp with sweat. He should wipe it, make her more comfortable, but getting her to the well where he could summon help was more important.

'I'm going to check the dilatation of your cervix,' he told her, brushing his hand across her cheek because he couldn't say all the things he wanted to say to her, not now when he had to concentrate on her welfare, not his feelings. 'If it's not too dilated, I'll drive you to the well. I can contact the hospital from there and get a helicopter to collect you.'

She pressed her hand over his and nodded her thanks, biting her lip, so he knew another contraction was on the way.

He also knew that they wouldn't get to the well.

What did he have with him? An emergency kit in the car—it would have scissors that would be useful to cut the cord but little else as far as he could remember.

Water—he'd have plenty of water.

Think!

The mental order slowed his panic, and he found more damp napkins in a sealed container and used one to wipe Liz's face. She smiled at him and he thought his heart might break, then she whispered, 'You *do* remember how to deliver a baby!'

The gentle tease was worse than the smile, as far as affecting him went, but just in case she wasn't teasing he was quick to reassure her.

'Of course!' he said, then teased her back. 'I'm already boiling water on the fire, although I've never been quite sure what the boiling water you read about it stories was for. Maybe to sterilise the scissors.'

He kissed her lightly on the cheek and added more seriously, 'I'm going to the car. I'll be right back.'

He left the damp napkin with her and made sure she was comfortable on the couch, then headed for the car, finding the first-aid kit easily, and the drum of water, which he took with him, although Saif had left plenty in the tent.

He returned to find she'd moved, and was standing, gripping the tent pole.

'Better this way,' she gasped through pain, and he remembered his grandmother telling him how she had given birth, squatting while she gripped a solid pole set in the ground.

He held Liz while the contraction racked her body, so much stronger now that he wondered she could stand it, but as it passed she leant back into him and, holding her in his arms, a weird kind of happiness, something he'd never felt before, pulsed through his veins and calmed his panicked mind.

Though not for long! As Liz's labour continued, at what seemed to him an alarmingly rapid rate, he wished he could remember more about childbirth. His obstetric days, back when he had been a student and an intern, were long behind him, and any knowledge he'd ever had about a situation like this had to be retrieved from a long-unused part of his brain.

What he did know was that he had to be ready—ready to handle a fragile, newborn baby. He searched the tent, found clean headscarves and a clean kandora, thanks to Saif, who believed his master should never appear with a spot on his clothing or the wrong crease in his headdress.

Leaving the kandora—he could put that on Liz later—he piled the other things he might need on a towel beside where Liz now squatted, her hands still gripping the pole, so involved with the process going on within her body he might as well not have been there.

A baby catcher, that's all he was—yet even as he had the thought, new excitement shafted through him. He was going to deliver Liz's baby!

Well, she'd do all the work, he'd just be on hand—but now the tension in his body was different, more like elation than panic. He held her again, squatting behind her so his arms could support her, talking to her, encouraging her, whispering things he doubted she'd remember later but words he wanted to say.

He felt the moment she began to push and sat behind her, his hands, washed and rewashed, ready for the arrival. He felt the head as it crowned, disappeared, then crowned again, emerging fully, the little body twisting so the shoulders would come through the narrow passage, then with a final push the baby was in his hands and Liz had collapsed onto the blanket he'd spread beside the pole.

He stared at the baby, transfixed by her beauty and perfection, and smiled when she gave a cry that sounded full of resentment at being ejected from her sanctuary. She even blew a little bubble when he used a straw to clear her mouth and nose of mucus.

When he felt her chest moving as she breathed, he held the little bundle towards Liz.

'A little girl,' he whispered, his voice so husky with emotion the words croaked out.

But even in the dim light of the lantern he could read the despair in Liz's eyes and see the way her hands moved towards the tiny infant then were pulled back with what seemed an almost superhuman effort.

'Will *you* cuddle her for me?' Liz whispered, tears streaming down her face. 'Hold her against your skin for a few minutes and talk to her. She's used to men's voices.'

Liz's voice broke on the last few words and she turned away, her hand pressed against her mouth to stem the emotion she was obviously feeling.

He held the baby as she asked, glad he hadn't had time to dress so she could feel his skin, but his mind was on the woman, not the baby, for all she, premature as she was, should have all his concentration.

'Just keep breathing, *farida*, my precious pearl.' he whispered to the little girl, wrapping her carefully before setting her down to turn his attention to her mother.

How could this be so hard? How could she possibly be hurting more than she had during the brief labour?

The questions jostled with more practical matters in Liz's head and although she knew she should be gathering her wits and making sure Khalifa was doing all the right things for the baby, the ache of loss, so unexpected, was too overwhelming for her to think straight.

Perhaps if she held the little girl?

Then gave her up when Oliver recovered and wanted her?

She doubted she'd be strong enough to do that, knowing how much she already loved this infant, for all her determination to remain detached.

The bulge on her abdomen told her she was ready for the third stage of labour but it seemed Khalifa had remembered enough of his obstetrics training to have also recognised this fact. He'd set the baby, wrapped, it appeared, in one of his red-checked headscarves, quite close but not right beside her, and was preparing to deliver the placenta.

What must he be thinking of her? All he'd wanted was to share his delight in the desert with her, and here she was, causing all this trouble. And she had no doubt, knowing him as she now did, that he'd blame himself for the baby's premature arrival.

She wanted to say something, to thank him, but the words wouldn't come, because now something else had bobbed into her erratic brain and she was crying again.

'Liz?' His voice was gentle. 'Is it the baby? Do you want to hold her?'

Liz shook her head, swallowed hard, then poured out more grief on the poor man, knowing she shouldn't but unable to stop herself.

'It wasn't meant to be like this! They should have been here, and we were going to keep the cord and donate it for research. It was all planned.'

She knew her voice had risen to a pathetic wail, but Khalifa, who probably should have found an excuse to be busy elsewhere, was lifting her so he could take her in his arms, lifting her and carrying her outside, setting her down on the mattress where they'd made love—had it only been hours earlier?

'You've had so much pain—too much really for anyone to bear—but you are strong, Liz Jones, the strongest woman I have ever known. Yes, it hurts, but you've brought life to a new soul and now, if you look over there, you will see the sun coming up on a bright new day. You've seen desert sunsets, now watch the sun rise over a new day and know that we are given new days so we can start again and make each day better than the last one.'

He kissed her lips then left her, leaning back against the cushions, thinking of his words as she watched the slowly rising sun bring the desert to life.

Khalifa lifted the baby and, holding her cradled in one arm, walked out to the car, checking the crib they were carrying around. But there was no way he could see to secure it in the vehicle so back at the tent he packed one of the picnic baskets with towels, making a nest for her for before settling her into it. Once sure she was secure, he carried the basket out to the car where he strapped it in as tightly as he could, using a seat belt.

He'd already mentally debated asking Liz to hold her, but had decided that was probably less safe than his makeshift baby capsule. One abrupt stop and she could fly out of Liz's arms.

He returned to Liz, sitting where he'd left her, watching the magic of the sunrise, her skin touched to gold by the reflection from the dunes, the slight smile on her lips enough to break his heart all over again, but this was not the time for emotion. He had a fragile premature infant to take care of, not to mention possible complications for Liz.

Heaven forbid…

'We must drive to the well,' he said, stifling any hint of emotion. 'I can radio for help from there.'

She nodded but didn't move until he bent to lift her.

'No,' she said, 'I'm quite capable of walking. I've been enough of a burden to you already. Besides, I need to go into the tent—to dress in something.'

He helped her to her feet, her hand in his, his arm supporting her, yet close as he was he knew he wasn't really there—not for her—some distance having grown between them, something having shifted in their admittedly brief and unlikely relationship.

Which was good, wasn't it?

'Then I must check the baby,' she said, confirming his impression, for she was back in Dr Jones the neonatologist mode, which left him where?

The chauffeur?

'You'll find a clean kandora in the tent, you can put that on,' he said. 'And plenty of water and towels.'

She walked away and as he watched the long slim legs beneath the slightly bloodstained tunic she still wore moving her away from him, a sense of loss invaded his soul.

What had she said?

She needed to check the baby?

He went to the car and released the seat belt, carrying the picnic basket into the tent where he could unwrap the little girl on a table.

Liz was standing there, his kandora looking far better on her than it did on him, but the pain he could see in her eyes and the lines of strain on her face told him this was going to be one of the hardest things she had ever done.

To examine her own child, yet not touch her with love.

'You are still her aunt—you can love her,' he said to Liz, wanting so much to ease her pain. 'And surely you love all the babies you examine—at least a little bit.'

Liz heard the words but for a moment they didn't sink in, and then, as her body relaxed and the hurt she was feeling grew less, she turned and smiled at the man who'd uttered them.

'It seems I keep having to thank you,' she said, still smiling as she looked down at the tiny baby.

Carefully she checked that all was well, guessing at the baby's weight, checking breathing and heart rate, stupidly counting toes and fingers—mother stuff—silly, really...

'She's all good but must stay warm.'

She wanted to suggest holding her, for warmth, not because her arms ached to do just that, but there were dangers in holding a baby in a moving vehicle.

'Here,' Khalifa said, handing Liz lots more towels. 'We can use these to wrap her in tightly'.

Together they settled the baby once again.

Together, Liz thought sadly. She had so enjoyed the togetherness they'd shared, every moment of it, but now—well, she could hardly expect the man to fall in love with a woman when he'd had to deliver her baby...

She watched Khalifa as he carried the picnic basket to the car, watching the care and concentration he gave to the task of securing it, surprised when he paused. Was he examining his handiwork? Checking everything?

But, no, he was studying the baby, for he smiled and reached into the basket, apparently to touch the tiny girl, his lips moving as if he was speaking to her.

Liz blinked away the tears, telling herself the cause was postnatal hormonal imbalance, not a longing to touch the child in just that way, to whisper to her—damn it all, *to hold her*!

She's Oliver's, she told herself, over and over again, but no amount of telling eased the pain.

'Ready?' Khalifa called to her, apparently surprised she wasn't in the car.

'Coming now,' she said, sniffing back the unshed tears

and gathering the remnants of her courage around her like a tattered cloak.

'Exactly how early is she?' Khalifa asked as he took his seat behind the wheel and started the engine.

'Four weeks, give or take a day or so,' Liz told him, then had to ask, 'Why?'

'I wondered if we should head for the well where I can call for a helicopter, or if it would be safe to drive back to Najme. It will take an hour to the well, then the helicopter will probably be there in three-quarters of an hour, and have you both back to the hospital half an hour after that.'

Liz added up the times, then realised he was telling her this for a reason.

'There's an alternative?'

He turned to her and smiled.

'We could drive. It would mean cutting across the desert but I've done it dozens of times and have a GPS. Driving, we could be in Najme in three to four hours. What do you think? Should she be airlifted because that's quicker?'

This is just another patient, Liz told herself. What would you decide?

The little girl's responses had been good, her breathing and heart rate fine, there was no reason she'd even need a special crib in hospital, so...

But was she, Liz, leaning towards the drive because she wanted more time with the baby, even if she wasn't holding her? Somehow, just knowing she was so close was enough at the moment, but at the hospital, someone else would care for her and she herself...

Well, what would *she* do?

What *could* she do?

Keep pretending it was just another baby, a patient like any other?

Her heart cried out in denial, but she'd been so good,

so strong in keeping faith with the fact that it wasn't her baby, she really, really didn't want to weaken now.

'I'll drive unless you tell me she really needs a helicopter.' Khlaifa's voice, gentle and understanding, broke into her silent debate. 'I can understand you wanting to have more time with her,' he added. 'For all you've denied any maternal instinct, it's only natural you wouldn't want to be separated from her.'

He turned his head towards her and she saw the smile that still started so much reaction in her body.

'*You* taught me that,' he said, then he reached out and touched her cheek, although his eyes were back on the sand across which they travelled. 'Taught me so many things.'

Like what? she wanted to ask, but perhaps it was better just to accept the compliment—to hold it to herself like a precious gift.

'What will you do?' he asked, his attention back on the trackless desert that stretched like an endless red ocean before them.

'Do?'

'In Namje,' he added. 'You'll need to be checked by an obstetrician, and you'd be welcome to stay on either in a hospital bed or in an on-call room, close to the baby.'

Close to the baby?

'Oh, Khalifa!'

His name came out on a sigh and she caught back the maudlin thoughts that once again threatened to overwhelm her.

'You're right, I'll see a doctor...' she had to smile for she was sitting right beside one, and was a pretty good professional herself '...then maybe an on-call room, not to be close to the baby but so I can get on with the work you brought me here to do.'

'Then stay at the palace. I'll make sure you have a car

and driver available at all times so you can come and go as you wish.'

She could hear the things he hadn't said—about the baby, and questions about why she was so adamant to stay detached.

'It's not just Oliver,' she whispered. 'If it was, I'd be okay because he'd want me to love the baby as much as he would. It's his parents. When Oliver regains consciousness he'll still be far from well, so his mother will be the baby's primary carer, and if she won't let me near Oliver, there's definitely no way she'll want me involved in the baby's life.'

She paused, trying to get all the permutations and combinations of the future that had jostled in her head since Bill's death into some kind of order. Khalifa, after all he'd done for her, deserved an explanation.

'I could push to keep her, or at least be allowed access, because legally, right now, she's mine. But I couldn't let her become a pawn in a tug of war between myself and Oliver's parents, particularly if Oliver never recovers completely.'

She turned to Khalifa and touched his arm.

'That's likely, as you know, after a head injury. And just think of the joy she'd bring him. A man, broken-hearted over his partner's death, broken in health as well, then suddenly there's this little girl, someone to live for, someone to love and cherish...'

She shook her head, sniffed back more tears and added, 'I couldn't take that away from him.'

Khalifa's heart was scrunched with pain for this woman who sat beside him, her own heart breaking so she could bring happiness to someone else. Someone she'd obviously loved, but still...

'Anyway,' she said, with false bravado, 'we'd settled

all that long ago. I'm just a bit emotional about it all right now, but I'll survive. And although the palace is a beautiful serene place, I'd be better off at the hospital. I found out from Laya there's a breast-milk bank already established at the hospital so I'll give milk to that. It doesn't matter if she gets my milk or someone else's as long as it's the good stuff. And she's big enough to go into the ordinary nursery, but if you could wangle Laya to look after her, I'd be very grateful.'

He'd been lost in wonder that she'd shifted so swiftly from the emotional to the practical when he heard her voice waver on the last few words. He stopped the car, unclipped his seat belt and turned towards her, putting his arms around her as best he could and holding her close against him.

'We'll work it out,' he promised, 'we, not you. You tell me what you want and you shall have it. I know you've had to rely on your own strength for a long time now, but do you think could you learn to lean on me, to let me help you in any way I can?'

He kissed her hair, mussed and sweaty, and rubbed his hands across her shoulders, rubbing at her back, offering comfort in the only way he could, with the physical caresses of a friend.

He felt her head nod against his shoulder and knew he'd have to make do with that for the moment. Right now he had to get them both to the hospital.

Easing her back into her seat, he started the car and they continued on their way. Fortunately the baby slept, for he'd have hated to imagine the emotional battle Liz would have had to fight if the infant had needed comforting or feeding.

Eventually the pink towers and minarets of Namje appeared in the distance.

'Another mirage?' Liz queried.

'No, that's the real thing,' he assured her, smiling because he knew from her voice she was feeling stronger now.

Could he really know her so well in such a short time, to be picking up intonations in her voice?

He knew he could, because it seemed he knew her in his bones, as if she was a part of him. How she felt about him was a total mystery, the arrival of the baby hardly a normal scenario for the morning after their first lovemaking.

And now his guilt returned. He'd let his passion for this woman put her and her baby into danger and although everything appeared to be working out all right, the guilt was still there.

The baby gave a cry as he turned into the hospital gates.

'She must know we've arrived,' Liz said, and although he'd seen her turn and her hand move as if to pat the child, she pulled back, biting at her lip, determined, he knew, not to give in to the welter of emotion that must be wrenching her to pieces beneath her composed demeanour.

He used his mobile to phone the hospital, although they were already in the drive, asking for Dr Hassan and explaining what had happened, requesting she be on hand to examine and admit the infant, asking her to get Laya to meet them. Then he contacted the hospital's head obstetrician, thankfully in the hospital at the moment, and explained about the desert birth.

'We'll go in the staff entrance, and Laya will meet us there to take the baby while I take you to a private room where you can be examined. I'm sure the doctor will want to keep you in as a patient at least overnight, and...' he turned and touched her cheek '...it would make me feel happier if you stayed at least that long.'

'I can hardly say no when you've been so good to me,'

Liz responded, but he knew the distance he'd felt between them at the campsite in the desert was growing stronger—a distance he had no idea how to breach.

Once examined and pronounced fit, Liz showered and changed into her own clothes, which had miraculously appeared while the obstetrician was with her. Pleased she knew her way around the hospital, she went down to the nursery where Dr Hassan assured her the baby was fine.

The doctor indicated the crib, although Liz hadn't needed to be told, for Laya was sitting beside it and Khalifa hovering over it.

She didn't want to see Khalifa—well, she could see him already—but she didn't want more conversation with him. This was partly because she already felt so beholden to him for handling her typical klutz-like emergency delivery, but also because something seemed to have shifted between them. The closeness she'd felt in the desert had whisked away like a sand sprite, lost for ever in another world.

Not that she could turn around and walk out...

'I've been passed all clear by your doctor,' she told him as she approached the pair beside the crib. 'In fact, he tells me you did a splendid job, so there you are. Perhaps a second speciality lies ahead for you.'

She sounded like a robot, rattling on about nothing, but standing here, seeing the little pink face of the child she couldn't call her own, was tearing her apart, and while she longed to lean into the strength Khalifa had offered, the something that had shifted between them held her back.

She mumbled some excuse and left the room, although she'd intended asking about the procedures in place for donating breast milk. She couldn't return to her hospital room and brood—madness lay that way—so she walked further down the corridor to where the alterations to the new neonatal unit were well under way.

Khalifa found her there and, thankful the workmen had all departed, he took her in his arms.

'Talk to me,' he said, as she had said to him after they'd made love.

'I don't know what to say, or what to think, or what to do,' she whispered. 'It's as if I'm waiting for a sign, waiting for something to happen that will tell me which way to turn.'

He didn't have an answer so he kissed her, because it seemed the next best thing, and holding her like this it was difficult not to kiss her. Her response suggested the coolness between them might have been in his imagination, but common sense warned him that he was holding a very emotionally fragile woman in his arms, and her response might have been nothing more than a desperate need for comfort.

He would keep on kissing her, just for a while, and if that was selfish, because his body had been craving to hold her, then so be it, and hopefully she'd get some solace from it as well.

Eventually she broke away, an experimental smile on her face, so pathetic he wanted to kiss it off.

'I made a mess of things as usual,' she muttered. 'Going into labour like that, ruining what should have been a perfect night.'

'Nonsense,' he said. 'What could be more perfect way to finish a night than the arrival of a new child?'

He kissed her again but this time there was no response, and she eased herself away from his body and didn't even try to smile as she whispered, 'Oh, Khalifa, I am just so confused at the moment, I don't know where to turn.'

Turn to me, he longed to say, but though he might not

have known her long, he knew she would have to work her own way out of her confusion. All he could do was be there for her.

For her and the baby...

CHAPTER ELEVEN

Liz returned to her room and, working out the time difference between Al Tinine and home, phoned Gillian to ask how Oliver was.

There had been no change. This information didn't help. Although she chatted to her friend for a few minutes, asking after the cat and the hospital, she didn't mention she'd given birth to Oliver's baby. If thinking about the baby made her teary, talking about her to Gill would have brought on an emotional tsunami!

'So, now what?' she said aloud in the empty room, but when she tried to think she realised her brain had turned to jelly and refused to cooperate.

Maybe if she slept…

She was a sand sprite, coming to life only at night. The darkness all around her told her it was night, so she moved, tentatively at first, feeling for limbs instead of whirling grains of sand, finding legs and arms and toes and fingers, realising she was alive.

Because it was night? Or because she'd made love to a human and been forced to stay alive for ever?

Wasn't that a good thing?

Yes, most definitely, when her body remembered the shivery excitement of their kisses, the languorous pleasure of the human's touch, the smoothness of the couch beneath them, the heat of his body curled into hers, his tenderness, the gasping pleasure as they climaxed, lying with him afterwards, held safely in his arms.

A prince. He was a prince, and beautiful, and staying alive meant she could love him for ever and he would love her, and so she'd have no regrets, would she...?

She woke with a start, the dream so vivid her body could feel the physical pleasure she and Khalifa had shared.

But he *was* a prince, and him loving her for ever was no more than a dream.

Restless now, she glanced at her watch. Past midnight—her body clock was all out of kilter again. But past midnight meant there'd be few people in the nursery. She could safely go and look—just look—at the baby. Oliver's baby.

She pulled on a gown and started down the corridors, past the windows to the outside verandas where the families of patients slept, and quietly into the nursery, moving unerringly towards the baby's crib, stopping when she realised the man asleep in the chair beside it was Khalifa.

Khalifa?

She backed away into a shadowy corner because the baby was stirring, and although the little one hadn't made a sound Khalifa must have sensed she was awake, for he straightened up and peered into the crib, then, smiling, lifted the little bundle into his arms, talking to her, rocking her, smiling all the time. The baby lay still, yet Khalifa didn't return her to the crib but held her in his arms, sitting down again, speaking so quietly Liz couldn't tell if it was in Arabic or English.

Liz crept away, more confused than ever.

Was the baby a replacement to him—for the daughter he had lost? If not, why was he doing this, sitting with her, holding her, talking to her?

Bonding!

She should go and ask him, but in truth she was glad the baby had someone holding her and talking to her, especially a male so she'd know the man smell of him.

But thinking of the man smell of Khalifa was dangerous when she was in this muddled state of mind, so she returned to bed and forced herself to count camels until she fell asleep. Although, she thought muzzily as she drifted off, she couldn't recall actually seeing a camel since she'd been here.

She spent the next day avoiding Khalifa, avoiding the nursery when she saw him there, spending time with Phil as they worked out costings for the new unit, and checking equipment that was already coming in. But it was hard to avoid him when she returned to her room to find not only Khalifa in it, but a crib, complete with baby, presumably the one she'd carried, though not hers, never hers.

Her eyes filled with tears and she cursed her own weakness, but Khalifa's attention was on the baby, so maybe be hadn't noticed.

She dashed them away with her hand and hardened her voice.

'What's this?'

He turned abruptly, as if caught out in wrongdoing, then smiled the smile that touched her heart every time she saw it.

Coming towards her, he took both her hands in his, guiding her to the bed and settling her on it, sitting beside her and curling his arm around her shoulders.

'Liz, there's been news and I had to tell you personally. But I didn't want to leave the baby so I brought her along as well.'

The words made so little sense Liz shook her head, but her eyes were darting towards the crib, towards the little pink and white bundle with a shock of dark hair lying, swaddled, in it.

Khalifa's arm tightened and his voice was deep and grave.

'Oliver is dead,' he said.

Shock held her silent but only for a moment.

'He can't be. I spoke to Gill last night.'

'I'm sorry, my love, but he is,' Khalifa responded. 'His parents decided to turn off the life support this morning.'

Although a little bit of her had grabbed those two words—*my love*—and clung to them, Liz knew she had to understand the real message, *and* the implications of it.

Implications that had started panic in her chest.

'But the baby? What about the baby?'

'We don't have to decide that right now,' Khalifa told her gently, 'but I rather hoped she might be ours.'

Confusion joined the panic.

'Ours?'

'Yours and mine, but we'll work that out later. Right now, do you want to hold her, nurse her, talk to her, think about a name?'

'But…'

Had he sensed her total confusion? For he left her sitting on the bed and went to the crib, lifting the baby, murmuring to it in a foreign language, the voice deep and soothing, switching to English as he took a step towards Liz.

'See, *farida*, precious pearl, this is your mother. I was telling you about her, and now she really can be your mother and hold you, just as I told you.'

Liz could only stare at him, but she held out shaking arms and took the infant, no longer concerned about the tears that flooded from her eyes and fell to dampen the tiny bundle's wrappings.

Khalifa stood and watched her, seeing the happiness

behind the tears, understanding the welter of emotion Liz must be going through. The loss of her friend, but the confirmation that the baby she'd carried so generously for her brother and his partner would now be hers.

If only he could take the pain away from her, carry it for her, help her through it.

If only he had the right.

He sat and held them both, a million thoughts flashing through his head, but paramount among them was the need to make this woman his—so that he and she and the baby would make a family and he *could* help her through her grief.

'She's eating well and sleeping well and needs no special care,' he told her. 'If we take Laya to help you look after her while you regain your strength, can we take her home?'

'Home?' Liz queried, turning to look at him, dampness from her tears still lingering on her cheeks so he had to touch her to brush it away.

He took a deep breath and plunged into what he later realised was a *most* prosaic and loveless proposal. But he had to get it said before his courage failed completely. The thought of losing this woman was so overwhelming he had to know where he stood.

'This is not the most romantic spot for what I want to say, but I don't know when there'll be another time for us to be together—just the three of us.'

He was frowning and Liz realised that his voice, for the first time since she'd met him, was slightly hesitant. Then he smiled, and while her body went into its usual reaction of delight, her brain told her that something important was coming up.

Tension built to snapping point as Liz waited.

And waited.

Now he tried for a smile, tightened his grip on her shoulders, and said, with a pathetic smile, 'How would you feel about marrying a bloke with more money than sense?'

Khalifa knew he was making a complete hash of this. The moment the words had come out he'd known they were wrong, but apart from yelling 'Marry me', which was what he'd most wanted to do, he'd not had a clue of how to propose.

No wonder Liz looked confused.

'M-m-marry you?' she stuttered. 'Why?'

'Because we like each other and we've got the baby. I've been bonding with her, like you said, and I can give you both a comfortable life, and you can still work if you want to, and you seem to like the country and the people you've met, and there's no one left for you at home—you told me that—and, besides, I'd like it.'

He had a vague feeling he'd made things worse but was still surprised by her reaction.

'Is this to do with guilt?' she demanded. 'Guilt about your wife and child dying, guilt about taking me out into the desert? I might not have known you long, Khlaifa, but I know how you treasure your guilt, piling it up inside you like the nomads pile their belongings on their camels.'

His turn to be stunned!

He tried to protest but she was speaking again.

'And would a replacement wife and child, no matter how well you've bonded with the child, ease that guilt?'

'Liz, no, believe me, that's not true.'

She eyed him with suspicion written clearly on her face, but when she spoke it was to comfort him. She took his hand and used both of hers to hold it.

'It wasn't your fault your first wife died,' she said gently. 'You know that. As for me, the scorpion stung me because I was there and I was careless. I knew about scorpions and should have shaken out my clothes before putting them on, so you don't have to marry me out of guilt, okay?'

'I didn't offer out of guilt,' he muttered at her, annoyed now that something he'd thought would be so easy was turning into a nightmare.

'Then why did you offer?' she demanded, her blue eyes behind the horror glasses so huge he could have drowned in them.

'I told you,' he said desperately. 'We're good together, I already love the baby, you like my country, there are plenty of reasons for us to marry.'

For a moment he thought those eyes had filled with tears but she turned away from him before he could be sure, looking out the window, her shoulders lifting with a sigh that seemed to echo around the desert beyond the car.

'No!' she said, just *no*, nothing more, sitting there, not even looking at him.

He stood up and began to pace the room, trying to work out how things had gone so disastrously wrong.

Would asking why help?

Not if her answer was she didn't love him.

In fact, that would make things worse.

Then he asked anyway, because he had to know.

Just one word—why?

Liz beckoned him back to sit beside her before she began to speak.

'You gave a lot of reasons for wanting to marry me,' she said, thinking through each word because she knew she had to get it right. 'But not the one I wanted to hear—the one I needed to hear.'

She moved and touched her hands to his face, cupping it and looking into his eyes.

'I know it will probably sound stupid to you, Khalifa,

but all my adult life I've known the one thing I wanted out of marriage, and that wasn't money, or a job, or even a palace. Just love. I wanted love like my parents had, like Oliver and Bill's. Mutual love that transcends all else, that distracts you at the most inconvenient time, that maddens and annoys and makes you ache when your loved one isn't near. You told me of the sand sprite and somehow made it sound as if she regretted making love to her human lover. But if she loved him there'd have been no regrets. There *are* no regrets with love.'

He put his hands on hers where they still rested on his face, his heart so full he doubted he could speak.

But speak he must.

'You don't love me?' he asked, and to his surprise she laughed.

'Oh, Khalifa,' she whispered. 'If you only knew how much! I love you to distraction and probably have since soon after we first met. But that's not enough. It has to be returned, or our life would be like a see-saw with one of us always up and the other always down, never balanced.'

'And you think it's not returned?' he murmured, and now he took her face in hers and kissed her lips, claimed them, consuming her with kisses.

'You say I've driven you to distraction since we first met, but you…!' he murmured against the soft skin of her neck. 'You've blown my mind, you've turned my life up-side down, you've got me in such a state the whole country could have fallen apart, so absorbed I've been in you. Then when you went into labour, I panicked that something would go wrong and I would lose you. Yes, I did feel guilt—but most of all I felt pain. Then I delivered your baby and it was as if heaven had given me a gift. I thought if I offered you a wonderful life for you and the baby you might stay here, but I should have known you better. Love? Of course I love you. More than I can ever say, more than you could ever know, always and for ever.'

'But you didn't think to mention it in your proposal?' she teased.

He rested his hands on hers and tried to explain.

'I was—I suppose scared sounds stupid, but that's what I was. Terrified more like—because after all it's just a word but...'

He couldn't do it, not sitting here so close, so he stood again and paced.

'I'd never realised quite how powerful a word it was, but even thinking about saying it made me feel vulnerable, and I doubt I'd ever felt that way before. Even when I was a child in the desert, or at boarding school. I'm a sheikh, with a long line of tough warriors behind me. We cannot be vulnerable. What if you hadn't loved me back—how much more vulnerable would that have made me? I know this must sound strange to you, but when I told you I loved you just now, that's the first time I've ever used the word—in English or in Arabic.'

She held out her hand to him and he drew her up and wordlessly they held each other, together protecting the vulnerability of love.

CHAPTER TWELVE

THE toddler went straight to the fountain, standing on tip-toe to splash her chubby little hands in the cool water, splashing Khalifa, who hovered over her, ready to catch her when her excitement brought her crashing down, as it inevitably would.

'A klutz, like her mother,' he said fondly, still waiting for the fall but turning part of his attention to the woman who lay back in a lounger beneath a nearby peach tree, the bulge of her pregnancy obvious beneath the fine cotton gown she wore.

'Demanding, like her father,' Liz countered, when her daughter grabbed Khalifa's snow-white kandora in her wet hands and scrunched a patch of it while yelling his name—or the Da, Da, Da she called him.

Farida Olive Wilhemina bin Khalifa al Zahn was prat-tling up at her father, and both Liz and Khalifa knew ex-actly what she wanted, which was to be stripped off and lifted into the water, where she would immediately fall over and emerge yelling her indignation.

'No,' Khalifa said, very firmly, but Liz could see he was already shuffling out of his sandals and hitching up his kandora, and in a minute would climb into the foun-tain himself so he could hold his daughter—the precious pearl he'd named her—while she splashed.

The year had passed so quickly. Settling into life at the palace, life as a mother, life as Khalifa's wife—this last made her body burn, pregnant though she was—had made the time pass quickly, but at last Liz felt at peace. Thinking of the loss of Bill and Oliver would always cause a little ache inside her, but the gift they'd given her, this beautiful little girl, eased it immensely, while the gift of Khalifa's love had made her complete in some way she could never explain, even to herself.

He turned towards her now, as if drawn by her thoughts, and smiled. Her toes curled and inside the sparks and fizzing was just as bad as ever.

Or as good as ever...

'The sand sprite would have had no regrets,' she said to him, and knew he understood.

* * * * *

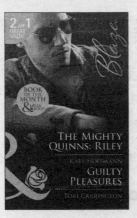

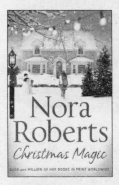

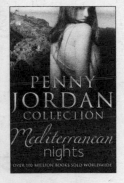

The World of Mills & Boon®

There's a Mills & Boon® series that's perfect for you. We publish ten series and, with new titles every month, you never have to wait long for your favourite to come along.

Blaze®

Scorching hot, sexy reads
4 new stories every month

By Request

Relive the romance with the best of the best
9 new stories every month

Cherish™

Romance to melt the heart every time
12 new stories every month

Desire™

Passionate and dramatic love stories
8 new stories every month